Nathanial Goldsmith is the only son of the richest man in the Idaho territory, Jessum Goldsmith, the Silver Baron of the Western Lands, as he is called in all the newspapers. But life in the late nineteenth-century American West weaves no magic spell for Nathanial, who longs for the academic worlds his father has forced him to leave behind.

To toughen him up, Nathanial's father has indentured him to a ranchman, Cayuse Jem, a large, raw-boned, taciturn man Nathanial's father believes will help teach his son to "become a man." Cut off from his books and the life he has always known, Nathanial is not only forced to co-exist with Cayuse Jem, but to truly get to know him. In doing so, Nathanial discovers there is more to this silent horseman than meets the eye. And, in the process, Nathanial also learns a few things about life, about human nature, and about the differences in being a man and a boy...

THE

BIBLIOPHILE

Drew Marvin Frayne

A NineStar Press Publication

Published by NineStar Press
P.O. Box 91792,
Albuquerque, New Mexico, 87199 USA.
www.ninestarpress.com

The Bibliophile

Printed in the USA
First Edition
November, 2018

Print ISBN: 978-1-949909-46-3

Also available in eBook, ISBN: 978-1-949909-43-2

Warning: This book contains sexually explicit content, which may only be suitable for mature readers, and the off-page death of a secondary character.

21 June 1888

I HAVE NOT kept a journal since I was a boy. I last abandoned these pages during the inverse leg of this very journey, four years ago, when I left the territory to go to school. It is perhaps ironic I kept no written record of these last four years, for when I am withered and old I suspect my time in school is the period in my life I shall look back upon with the most fondness and longing.

Instead, errant fool that I am, I have only kept a record of my daily comings and goings when I am at home, mired in the tedium of life in the territory. It should be considered a tremendous irony that I have maintained records of my existence only during periods of my life when it was not worthy of record. This journal is nothing more than an exercise in keeping at bay the stultification and mental weariness I know will come upon me once I return to that world, to the territory, and to time spent with my father. My existence there—all that I shall experience—it is beyond languor, beyond ennui. Life at my father's home represents nothing less than the atrophy of the mind itself.

Not that my father is a wicked man; I wish to impress this fact most sincerely, especially since it is probable that, in her "exploration" of my belongings, my grandmother is likely to uncover this diary and read these passages, and will hasten to share with my father any negative report she finds contained herein. No, my father is a good man, but a hard man, and a plain one—even Grandmomma must confess to that. The trappings of the world I hold most dear—those things that mean the world to me, those things that are my world, that define my world, that define me—they mean nothing to him. And even more painfully, my father has already determined the manner in which the arc of my life will bend, and I, his only son, must dutifully obey.

How I wish it were not so! After three years at preparatory school, I had completed but one year of my university studies. Yet I needed just one week—nay, one day, one hour—to know I truly belonged there, in Cambridge, in academe, in amongst those ancient tomes and dusty halls. Feldspar, my one friend at Harvard, used to josh me frequently and oft would say, "Goldsmith, you will lose yourself in the library someday, I guarantee!" And then he would laugh in that short-pitched bark of his, his laugh that always made the other fellows snigger as well. But I did not laugh. Rather, how I longed for what he said to come true. There, in the library, to read and study under the gas-lit lamps for as long as I wished, to be lost amongst the books... Yes, that is where my heart's desire can be found, as the old poem starts.

But what good will it do me? My father has but one son, and when you are the son of Jessum Goldsmith, your lot in life is naught but to obey. "Time to give up the books," he wrote me, his only letter in the four years I was away from his custody. I had not to read his words at all to know what his communication meant to convey, to know it was a summons, and not the heartfelt correspondence of father to son. "Time to come home. To learn the business. Time to be a man." All my life I have longed for nothing more than books and words and worlds that unfurl one page at a time. I was meant for academe. I had hoped to complete my baccalaureate and continue straight on, for my postgraduate, for my master's, and then—my most sincere wish—to teach. To be forever a part of those hallowed halls. What care I for business and industry? But no, I am son to Jessum Goldsmith, richest man in the territory, and I do not have the freedom others of my age and station possess. How I wish I were a second son, or third, a son of lesser value and importance. But Momma died giving birth to me, and since I stole Father's past, I cannot steal his future as well.

"To be a man." Those words have haunted my existence since I have existed. My father measures manhood in far different ways than the professors I idolized, the masters whose learning captivated me and whose lectures I would listen to in spent and utter rapture. A man of letters, an intellect, someone who wrestles with ideas—to me, that is a man—that *defines* a man. Milton is a man. Donne. And Jonson and Pope and so many more, and that is just amongst the English. But my father is not a book-learned man, and his idea of what a man should be neither begins nor ends in the printed pages of any text. He was born to the outdoors, and me to the indoors, but rather than simply acknowledge our differences, he only tolerated them until such time as I turned eighteen, when he summoned me home for his tutelage to begin, and for my real "education" to commence.

Father's letter was accompanied by one from Grandmomma, a more faithful correspondent all these years, though, as ever, only a mouthpiece for my father. "You must come home, Nathanial," she wrote to me. "It is time to plan for the future. It is time to give up your books. Your family needs you. You must come at once." I could hear the gloat in every word. For so long I had begged to be sent East, to study, first in boarding school, and then at university. Father gave in, I believe, just to quiet me, and because, at such a young age, I held little use for him. But there, in Boston, I could live as I wished, with my books, and in my mind, alone and quite content to be so. I could be literate and educated and revel in such things as befits a learned man. But Grandmomma never saw the need for such lofty education and told me as such in almost every letter she sent. Yes, like the son she bore, she ever wrote in declarations, though that is the usual state of the world in her eye; every letter she sent to me reflected duty, honor, and obligation to my father and his ideals of masculinity, and, of course, to the vaunted Goldsmith name. Vaunted, indeed. I happen to know my Grandfather Goldsmith was a dry goods salesman from Michigan. It was my father, his son, who went into Idaho as a lad and made his fortune in the mines. Our name is no more hallowed than the tradesmen who gave it to us in the first place. A smith, after all, is one who works with precious metals, not one who possesses them. Our name should be a reminder of the humble beginnings of our family and the promise that a man may make his own way in this world. But no, to Grandmomma, to Father, we are the first family of the territory. We own the largest manor; we hold the most land; we possess the most wealth. It is all that matters to them.

I suppose I should find it ironic our name is Goldsmith; Father, after all, made his fortune in mining silver. "The Silver Baron of the Western Lands." That is what they call him in the Eastern newspapers. How oft would I read of his latest coup. And then the other fellows would stand around me and ask, "Is that truly your father, Goldsmith?" As if they did not know. But most of them—Fulton, Hardwicke, Matthews, and the like—all they cared about was money, too. Only Feldspar understood how little it meant to me. Only Feldspar understood that what I cared about was the books, the words, and the ideas contained within. Those were the worlds that meant so much to me. Not money, not industry, and certainly not mining. Just the words. How I longed to be part of that world, to be part of the discourse of scholarship and books and ideas. It is in my disposition to be of that world.

It is who I was meant to be.

Or so I always believed.

But then again, of what consequence are my own beliefs and ideals?

I doubt I shall ever see Feldspar again. I had not thought of that until now. I suppose I should feel disconsolate over that but...truly, I feel nothing. Perhaps I am simply resigned to my fate. Perhaps I am incapable of such feelings, or feeling anything but for my books. I have never had many friends, and those I do are such friends of the sort one exchanges pleasantries with, and not the sort one shares one's innermost confidences and expressions. Even Father, hard man that he is, has Abernathy, his lieutenant, with whom he plots and plans for the future, for the next mine or the next land grab or the next political power play. I have no one. Then again, perhaps I need no one. I fear I do not have any such innermost desires for companionship.

All I have ever truly cared about are my books.

Well, and, of course, Dora. My sister. Older by a year. A carefree child, though, I suppose, no longer a child. Her letters mean almost as much to me as my tomes. And while I am sure she did not care to receive my surely dull correspondences of what I had been reading and what I had been learning, she always paid attention and always asked her little brother to tell her more. And oh, how she loved to hear of Boston, of the Old North Church and the Quincy

Market Hall and the teeming masses of people from all walks of life and corners of the nation—indeed, the world. Oh, she herself never expressed any desire to see it. That is not her way. But at Christmas I would send her etchings I purchased from the booksellers of the sights of the city, and she always wrote that she felt as if she had glimpsed it for herself. Yes, it will be good to see her again, to walk with her amongst the gardens and whisper conspiratorially about Father's demanding ways. But that does not counterbalance the loss of school. And she will be wed soon, I would wager, and then she will be gone as well.

The train is stopping presently, as we are pulling into Chicago. Perhaps I will disembark and stretch my legs. Our family car affords me every luxury and every privacy, but the only other soul I have seen since leaving Boston is Cheevers, our man, and dull sort that he is, he has done nothing but sit in a corner and stare blankly afore, pausing infrequently in his ruminations to serve tea. I asked him, as we pulled out of Philadelphia, what he might be pondering so deeply, but the question seemed to puzzle him most earnestly, so much so that I gave up any hope of an answer. Yes, I think I shall disembark upon Chicago and perhaps converse with a fellow passenger or two, at least to exchange a pleasantry or any news of the journey. And possibly—one can hope—there will be a bookseller at the station. It will be three more days before we reach Boise. And two more after that to home, if the roads are good. Something new to read would gladden my heart indeed.

28 June 1888

I HAVE BEEN home two days and the situation is far worse than I feared. Dora *is* to be married—and to Abernathy. For a man who hates book learning, this decision of my father's seems to derive from some aged history of those medieval rulers who married their daughters off with little consideration of their feelings or delicacy. My poor sister. Her entire life she has had but one desire—to be wed, to raise children, to have a happy domestic existence. This she will not find with Abernathy. Yes, the man is wealthy—he owns vast swathes of the northern forest. But he is twice her age and has the pallor, countenance, and disposition of a winter weasel. I fear she will be unhappy in life. Yet what can either of us do? Her lot is to be wed, sold off in an exchange of assets. Her happiness is no more a concern of Father's than my own. Such is the fate of the children of Jessum Goldsmith.

As for me, well, Father does not need me to run the mines—no, indeed, and why should he? He has men for that. No, he wishes me to learn the business only to present us both as captains of industry, so he may achieve his own political leanings.

Bah! Politics! At least in running the business, I would have my own freedoms and could spend my leisure hours as I wished. But Father has loftier ambitions for me. Grandmomma told me as such the instant I returned. "Nathanial," she said, "finally, you are home. You should never have left. But there is still time."

"Time for what, Grandmomma?"

"Idaho will be a state soon. Your father will be made senator. You must be by his side. But in order to do that, you cannot be as you are. You must learn, now, before it is too late, to be a man of the world."

Ahh, to be a man of the world. That old refrain. How oft have I read these same words in the letters she sent. "Books and learning," she would write, exhorting me to come home, "are for boys and well-born women." I was not the tall, strapping vision of masculinity her own son reflected. I was never what they demanded of the only son of Jessum Goldsmith. My own father put it more directly to me the evening of my arrival. "You will not be able to govern," he said, "not here, not in the West, from what you learn out of books. No, it must come from there," he added, pointing out the window to the wider expanses beyond. "From there you will learn how to govern this territory. This state. And perhaps, given time..." He left the thought unfinished, but it showed how far-ranging his ambitions were for me. For him, truly, I should say, not for me.

I had no interest, none at all, in any of this. But I thought, perhaps, in my naiveté, I could turn his ambitions to my advantage. "Father, though, if you wish me to go into governance, is it not wise that I receive a university education first? If not back East, then there are schools in California I could attend."

"Son—"

"Or perhaps even here in the territory?" Now my desperation was showing. "There is a college in Caldwell. It is small and no university, but it may suffice. Or, I am given to understand they are opening a university up north. Perhaps I could—"

"No!" my father thundered, slamming his fist against a table. "I will hear no more talk of learning. I will hear nothing more of universities and books." With a sneer, he turned on me. "Is this what you wish to become? A sniveling scholar? A bibliophile locked away in a dust-filled room?"

How I longed to answer him "yes." But I wisely held my tongue.

"When I was your age," he continued, "I had already spent four years working the land, panning for gold, prospecting. My knuckles bled each night from the gravel I sifted and ached from the icy cold of the mountain streams. I trembled from the frost as I slept in the open air. I toiled. I suffered. It made me who I am."

Father's words made me think of the medieval mystics I had studied in Professor Cornwall's course last autumn, mystics who spoke of bloody wounds and unrepentant pain in the way another man might speak of a lover—fervently, and with great appreciation. Father may lack their eloquence, but he matched them in his zeal. I was soft, I suppose, if I found the tales of such activity lacking in appeal. I saw little point in glorifying occurrences that were uncomfortable and miserable when experienced; suffering with such lofty accord never seemed to truly come with any gain. For all it did for my father, for as rich and respected as he had become, I could not say it made him a happy man.

Sharing these thoughts, though, would only heighten my father's entrenched dissatisfaction in the sole male fruit of his loins. All my life, I could feel his disappointed eyes on me; now was no exception. My father is tall, broad shouldered, a self-made man. And I, his only son, am slight, studious, and effete. He likes power, and I like books. Small consolation indeed for a man who insisted the world be shaped in his own image.

But then again, reshaping the land is how my father won his fortune. And if he could do it to the very earth, then, I suppose, he trusted he could reshape me into a figure worthy of his mettle.

Perhaps I should have spoken out. I wish I had. I wish I had argued more forcefully. I wish I had said something. Perhaps Father would have respected that. But it is not my nature to be combative, to argue. And the only response I would obtain in return would be silence or ridicule or the back of his hand. No, these recriminations are but the wishes of a weak man. Not even a man, if my father and Grandmomma are to be believed.

Perhaps they are right.

30 June 1888

IT IS NOT to be the mines for me, after all; unlike so many poor souls in the antiquities of Titus Flavius Josephus or Dionysius of Halicarnassus, my fate is not meant to be sealed that way.

Conceivably I can still work my way up to it. I rather think my father would enjoy the sight of me with pickax in hand, one ankle chained to a wall, digging through the bedrock for precious ore. Is that how silver is mined in this modern day and age? I suppose I should know, but I do not. Perhaps I will learn, ere my father's tutelage is through.

But no, it will not be the mines for me, at least not in the beginning. Father deems, instead, to start me off small. I am to be a groom—or, rather, a groom's assistant, of a sort. A groom's groom? Father is a man oft found on horseback, and he believes riding is both a fundamental skill and an ardent pastime. There is a man who lives on the edges of our land who raises Appaloosa for Father to sell. I am to be his, at least for the time being.

I know a little something of the breed. They originated in this area; they were bred by the Nez Perce, who lost all of their horses in the War of 1877. (I bet Father did not know that! See, one can learn from books, even on such topics as animal husbandry.) Their distinctive coats make them popular in rarified circles back East, and Father sells the beasts to wealthy acquaintances for the equestrian shows that are so popular in Philadelphia, Boston, and New York.

But truly, I cannot imagine Father's passion stems from the money they bring him. No, he enjoys the contest with the horse. He likes to watch the animal broken, to see its spirit and resolve yield to his own. It is his way with all things. To own, to tame, to break; to possess or to destroy; this is how my father meets the world and seeks to bend it to his will.

It seems I have something in common with these dumb animals then.

But I am not to work in the stables connected to the main house; no, no soft bed for me in the evening. That would not do for my father; that will not toughen me up or make me into a man. I will live, I am told, in a wretched shack, and I will work for the slovenly man who raises and trains these horses for my father. I will feed the horses, fetch water and—my father seemed particularly delighted with this last bit—shovel their excrement, all day and all night. He feels quite sure it will be the making of me.

Indeed.

My library was locked away. The only book I am to be allowed is this accursed journal, so that I may record my progress. I should have argued. Fought. Perhaps even run away. But I did what I always do, what I always knew I would have to do.

I obeyed.

Tomorrow, I meet my jailor.

1 July 1888

MY JAILOR'S NAME is Angus Malcolm James Mackenzie, but my father, and everyone, it would seem, calls him Cayuse Jem. When I asked my father why he called the ranchman "Cayuse Jem," the only response I received was a sneer and my father telling me, "I guess some things aren't in your books after all."

Cayuse Jem is, as feared, a large, raw-boned, red-faced, slovenly man. A Scotsman, he is taciturn, aloof, and imposing.

I can see why Father likes him so.

Cayuse Jem's house is a ramshackle affair, though it is not one room as I feared—it is two. There is a great room accommodating a rather dingy table and two wooden chairs, a stone fireplace, and a black, smut-encrusted potbellied stove for cooking. A lesser chamber features a bed and a small wooden chest. When I inquired as to where the lavatory may be, Cayuse Jem's only response was a thumb pointed in the general direction of the outdoors.

If living in squalor is, indeed, the making of a man, I surmise I shall be fit to depart here in a week.

I had occasion to meet Scotsmen while in Boston, and as a rule, I found them friendly, garrulous, and inclined to drink. Cayuse Jem would appear to possess none of these qualities. If I had my books, I would not mind the quiet so much; indeed, I would prefer it. But I am bereft of even this simple pleasure; and so I must endure the silence.

Cayuse Jem is a large man, but not fat; burly, I should say, though I cannot imagine him throwing his bulk on or off a horse with any sense of speed or alacrity. Indeed, he does not seem to be in a rush about anything. And he has the most peculiar-colored hair, a sort of russet shade of red, made all the more peculiar by the fact that the vast majority of it emanates from his chin, in a wide, thick beard that seems capable of housing all manner of small creature. The hair on his head is shorn rather close to the skull—what hair is left—though the veritable girth of his beard suggests he is attempting to compensate for the patchier components on the top of his head. I imagine, side-by-side, the two of us would cut quite a figure: Cayuse Jem with his large beard and belly and red hair and me, pale and small and smooth-chinned, with hair as dark as velvet, like my mother before me. An odd duo, to be sure.

When we met, he had but one word for me: "Boy." Only my father calls me that, and so, instinctually, I replied in the same manner as I do for my father: "Sir." I cursed myself for this afterward. I may be sent here to work for this man, yet he is naught but a glorified ranch hand, and while I sometimes loathe my name, I am Nathanial Goldsmith, son of Jessum Goldsmith. I may not be a man in my father's eyes, but I am no one else's boy.

As I read over these last lines I have penned I find myself unsure who I am trying to convince with such brashness. Cayuse Jem? My father? Myself? Sadly, I do not think I am capable of persuading any of those three with the conviction of such a posture—especially myself.

Tomorrow I begin my apprenticeship in earnest. I shall have to endure this, much as I endure the other aspects of my life here in the territory. The dullness of the task before me shall be no different than my life as it was ere I first left the territory. It will be different, yes; less civilized, for one. But the sort of civilization I have sought during my entire existence on this planet cannot be found anywhere here, in the territory, in my father's realm, or in my father's plans for my future, either immediate or long-term. So what difference, really, does it make, if I am to exist in the great manor house, or in some ranchman's ramshackle hovel?

My path is set. My future determined. I shall work for Cayuse Jem. And I shall work, yes, and work hard, and learn to bear this simple, rustic existence. It will not be forever.

Compared to all that awaits me, how difficult, truly, could this be?

2 July 1888

IT IS PERHAPS no surprise that my mind, in its wayward efforts to keep itself amused, kept turning again and again to the Greek legend of the great Heracles. I suppose, though, that standing ankle-deep in the *ordure* of horses lends itself to reminiscences of the Augean stables. I would I had a river or two whose course I could modify to aid me in my endeavors.

As promised, my day's work began with the shoveling of excrement, and it seemed to end in the very same manner—with dull, pedantic labor. Indeed, the entire day was a solid mass of work; there was little to define the passage of time or to mark the movement of the day except for the completion of one task and the commencement of another.

This is not to suggest I am putting in effort where Cayuse Jem is not. Indeed, he was up before me, and as I pen these few notes before the evening meal, he is assembling some type of stew for our repast.

Still, such work is hardly taxing mentally, and I find the lack of such stimulation the height of tedium. To pass the time, I began to reel through Heracles's labors in my mind and then progressed on to other works and texts. I had recited all of the Roman emperors and their dates and was moving on to the popes when Cayuse Jem bade me come for the midday repast.

I must add, to make all demonstration of due fairness, that Cayuse Jem did show me a kindness or two today. He made sure I wore gloves; he checked my boots and gear to ensure it was proper for the work at hand. He also "introduced" me to some of the horses—that was his word, though I was unsure how one "shook hands" with a horse. I told this to Cayuse Jem, a minor witticism to ensure friendly relations between us, but I only earned a silent stare for my efforts.

Perhaps it was all my small attempt at humor had earned.

But I could see that Cayuse Jem used a gentle hand on the horses. And they are beautiful creatures. Though I had read about the breed, the sight of one—striking in its dappled array of black and white—far outstripped the scant descriptions I found in the few books I owned on the natural world. There was one horse, by the name of Palouse, that came directly to Cayuse Jem when he first appeared. Cayuse Jem stroked the horse's nose and whispered something to it I could not quite hear; I was surprised by this gesture, as I could not imagine my father treating an animal, or even a person, in any similar capacity. Cayuse Jem slipped it something from his pockets—a sugar cube, he later told me—and then patted it on its hindquarters to send it back to the rest of the herd.

Nonetheless, I am counting down the days to when this accursed "lesson" ends. I do not understand at all what it is my father believes this man can teach me; and even after one day, I would wager that the mental tedium is causing my gray matter to decline. Then again, coming back to the territory had already commenced that process; yet I fear being here, with Cayuse Jem, will hasten the disintegration of my higher functions.

4 July 1888

TODAY MAY BE the day one traditionally celebrates the independence of this nation, but I feel as though mine has been wrenched from me. I have been indentured to a man whose only directive in life is to work, and who expects the same of me.

Did I truly write anything kind about Cayuse Jem in my previous entry? I take it all back. There is no part of my body—not one small component—that is not wracked with ache as I pen these lines. In the past three days, I have labored as I never have before. I have shoveled excrement, yes, piles and piles of it, but that is the least of my toils. I have swept stalls, polished tack, and fetched pail after pail of water—pail after pail!—until my limbs felt ready to flee from my torso for their own sake and sanity. It is fitting, indeed, that my mind keeps wandering to the tale of Heracles and his many woeful labors.

I pondered if some form of protest might be in order. This toil is truly excessive! But what good would it do me? And Cayuse Jem is a large man, and strong; any protest, I am sure, would be met with violence. That is how my father would react, and such activity would only act to further aggrieve the situation.

I wish to add that I do not think of myself as indolent— not at all. At school, I would practice my recitals over and over until every component of each of them was perfect. But I am unused to such physical labor, and I find myself so exhausted by day's end that I fall into sleep before I fully settle into my bed. "Bed," perhaps, is not quite the most precise term for it. Cayuse Jem sleeps in a bed, a small, homemade affair located in the diminutive space off of the ranch house's great room. I sleep in a pile of straw covered by an old horse blanket of Indian design at the foot of his bed. A temporary situation for a temporary hand. How the mighty have fallen, as the old prophet says.

At least I am too fatigued to grieve for my lost books.

I am unsure what it is I am supposed to be learning from this tutelage. If I am pupil, then I feel as though I am being trained to be a fishwife. Whatever shall I learn next—how to cook for Cayuse Jem?

5 July 1888

PERCHANCE I AM the old prophet of which I recently wrote, for, indeed, I seem to have foretold the future: today I *was* obliged to cook for Cayuse Jem.

At dawn, I am expected to fetch water while Cayuse Jem prepares a simple breakfast, usually whatever eggs he finds in the small hen house attached to his barn. Today, though, I was sent for the eggs and told to prepare them while Cayuse Jem fetched the water.

Initially, I felt a sense of relief to not make the trek to the cold-running stream from whence I must obtain our drinking and washing provisions. But while I have scant experience with the manual labors I have thus performed for Cayuse Jem, I have never cooked a morsel in my life, nor even watched as my own meals were prepared. Even when collecting the eggs, my inexperienced and, dare I say, clumsy fingers dropped three, leaving only another three to suffice for our morning repast. I knew to place the pan on the heat but did not know how expertly the fire would warm the entirety of the pan, handle included, leaving myself with a vibrant red line down the center of my palm. And I knew enough to shell the eggs, but did not comprehend how difficult a task that could be. If they are meant to be opened, I say, the hens should lay them with hinges, for much easier use.

The end result of my ministrations was a burnt, dry, and pitifully small dish of what had once been eggs. This was not mouthful enough for a man like Cayuse Jem, let alone for two. And I felt certain my failures would result in a violent outburst, perhaps even in physical punishment. So far I had been met mostly with silence by Cayuse Jem, but this was my first true failure. I heaped all of the eggs onto his plate and sat at the table in dread silence, awaiting his return.

When he did return, he lowered himself into his chair with nary a sound. He peered closely at my gross failure, and I awaited his harsh words, or worse. But he said nothing. Instead, he picked up his fork and pushed half of the eggs onto my plate. And then, still without uttering a word, he ate every last morsel, with nary a comment about the charred portions or the eggshells that permeated the dish. When we finished, I cleaned off the plates, and we carried about our business as usual.

I must say I was rather perplexed by his response, or rather his lack thereof. Even now, at end of day, I am mystified. Though I am surely too sleepy to think much more upon it. I shall consider it again tomorrow.

6 July 1888

AS I WAS shoveling excrement in the stables this morning, pondering again the life of Heracles (no matter where my thoughts embark upon the commencement of the day's toil, they seem of their own volition to always turn toward Heracles and his labors when I must bring shovel to hand), a sudden thought occurred to me. Heracles was a slave, given to King Eurystheus as penance for the murder of his wife and children. True, he had been driven mad by the vindictive queen of the gods, but the slaughter of such innocents deserves just punishment, no matter the cause. Yet while I have been given to Cayuse Jem in a similar fashion, to labor as directed, am I not the innocent in my own mythmaking? For what crime am I being punished? A desire to better myself? A desire to learn? A love for words? No, my real offense is deigning to hope for an existence different from what those around me would deem even worthy of consideration. My fault is failing to measure up to the expectations of men like my father and Cayuse Jem and others of their ilk who see little worth in books and learning and value only what they themselves know and can accomplish. I was being punished for their petty ambitions and their limited view of the world.

The more I pondered the injustice of my condition, the more I began to seethe. Why must I be forced to labor in this manner? My hands wracked with ache; my feet stung with each step; my back throbbed with a dull hurt that threatened never to abate. What in this condition should prove edifying? What was I to glean from all this? And while it is true I had no cause to complain about the manner of my warden—Cayuse Jem had treated me with deference, if not kindness—the very fact of my incarceration began to gnaw at me. I felt a tightening in my chest, a rising surge of bile that darkened my brow and fomented a spirit of revolt deep within. This was a new sensation for me. I had always done as directed; compliance was the natural state of affairs when one is a student, and even more when one is the son of Jessum Goldsmith. But I was neither of those things here. And this whole affair was, after all, my father's idea, not mine own. My consent was never requested nor proffered. The more I considered my plight the more it was, I felt, conditionally and unequivocally unreasonable and unfair.

Such grievance demanded a response.

I did not outright blame Cayuse Jem for my troubles— he was but taking advantage of the free labor offered—but he *was* a representative of my father in this circumstance. As such, acting as my father's agent in my forced labor meant any response would necessarily fall most heavily on his head. Labor. My mind then fell, with perhaps no small amount of petulant glee, on the *secessio pleibis* of ancient Rome. If my father wished me to experience life as a plebeian citizen, very well; I should fight back with the tools the Roman citizenry used when the patrician class leaned too harshly on their meager, hardscrabble lives.

I decided to commit a strike action.

I had read all about the Chartist movement while at school. I resolved to adopt their workers' consciousness—if the conditions of labor are unfair, then one must simply stop laboring. I shall cease my toil until my father is forced to come to the ranch and reckon with me himself.

I dropped the shovel in the stable and walked out to the small patch between Cayuse Jem's ramshackle house and the main set of stables. I stopped to take a long, satisfying draught of fresh water from the stores. Then I made my way to the center of the patch. There stood an old copper beech tree, its yawning arms stretching higher than any other for a mile around. With a triumphant and near-mutinous air, I threw my workman's gloves to the ground and sat myself heavily at the base of the tree, the shade of its leaves providing a welcome respite from the midmorning heat. In spring, the tree's leaves would be purplish in hue, a majestic sight to behold, I am sure; but now, in midsummer, its leaves were the deep virid color of edible greens. This was where I would make my stand, though I should be seated when I do it.

I waited with a giddy but apprehensive sense of anticipation. How would Cayuse Jem react upon spying me? He is a large man, and his taciturn, aloof nature suggested he might not react kindly to my newfound air of insubordination. I did not envision him shouting in response—the man barely spoke at all—and his large size and terse manner surely indicated a physical response. I steeled myself for such a possibility. If he were to bruise my face or blacken my eye, it would only provide more evidence for my father that my current situation was untenable, and even dangerous, to my well-being.

Perhaps a half an hour passed before Cayuse Jem spied me whilst coming from the large paddock toward the house, likely to begin preparation of the midday repast. I set myself and attempted to look as determined as possible, though my innards felt as if they were filled with the fluttering of one hundred butterfly wings. Cayuse Jem halted when he saw me, advancing slowly in my direction. I shook. The look on his face—to be honest, it was not at all what I expected. It seemed more a look of concern than anger, as if Cayuse Jem were worried I was prostrate from the heat or from exhaustion, rather than determined to address my current situation through a rather impulsive gambit. I must confess I felt a small pang of guilt, as I did not wish to cause the man concern, but then, remembering my mission, I set my jaw and steeled myself once more.

I laid out the course of action in my mind. I would not speak if spoken to; I would not move if asked. If Cayuse Jem grabbed me, forced me to move, well, I would not be able to stand against him, but I would not aid him in such endeavors, either. But none of that occurred, because the man said not a word to me. About halfway to me Cayuse Jem suddenly halted; his look of concern was replaced by another look, one I could not identify, and one that lingered but for a moment. Then his face resumed its habitual placidity. He placed his large hands on his hips and stared into my eyes for a moment. I did my best to return his glare with as much force and determination as I could muster. Then, without a word, Cayuse Jem turned and walked away from me.

I did not expect our—confrontation—to go as it did. I expected violence or questions or some kind of response rather than no response at all. My mind churned. Cayuse Jem is playing a kind of waiting game with me. That must be it. He will go into the house, I reasoned, prepare the noonday repast, and endeavor to tempt me with food. I determined to take no part in ingesting even the smallest morsel.

I would not be deterred.

But Cayuse Jem did not go into the house. Instead, he pivoted and went into the stables. Moments later, I heard the familiar sound of the shovel scraping against the dry earthen floor of the barn. Cayuse Jem was cleaning the stables—my appointed task. Without a word he simply took it upon himself to complete the task that had been appointed to me. I could not fathom this response. Why would he do such a thing? Of course, the stables must be cleaned; layman though I was, I knew unsoiled stables were vital to the well-being of the horses. But Cayuse Jem had me for that. Only I refused to work. And so, rather than argue with me or threaten me or strike me—as was his right—or even engage with me in any particular capacity, he simply went to work and began to perform those tasks that had been set out for me.

I waited. Surely this would not last. Thirty minutes. He must be hungry. And tired. An hour. He needed rest. He had labored tirelessly all morning as well. But he did not emerge from the barn. And as the minutes passed, all I continued to hear was the familiar sound of the shovel moving against the earthen floor of the barn, the shuffling of feet, and the mucking sound horse excrement makes when it lands upon the wooden slats of the cart.

I stood. I struck the dust from my pants. I retrieved my gloves. I walked into the barn. I went over to Cayuse Jem. I held out my hand.

Without a word, he gave me the shovel. Then, still saying nothing, he turned and strode out of the barn, returning to the day's work he had yet to complete.

7 July 1888

WHEN EVENING ARRIVES on the small ranch, the work largely comes to an end, much to my intense relief. This is when I most long to lose myself in my world of words. Instead, I find myself penning my thoughts in this accursed journal. For his part, Cayuse Jem often sits in his rocking chair and stares straight on. He does not take a pipe, like Father, nor does he engage in idle conversation. He simply gazes into the distance and ponders—well, I do not suppose I have any instinct as to what a man like Cayuse Jem must ponder.

Tonight, though, after sunset, our usual routine became disrupted when Cayuse Jem sent me to the stream with two pails and then, upon my return, with two more. Upon my return from the second trip, I understood the intent of these additional chores: Saturday night is for bathing.

Cayuse Jem carried a large tin-metal tub from out of doors and placed it in the center of the great room. He was boiling water on the stove and added this to the tub. Then he poured in the water I had just carried. I was sent for more pails, and more, until the tub was three-quarters full and the temperature satisfied Cayuse Jem.

My hands numb with ache, I went to retire to my straw bed, but Cayuse Jem spoke: "Stay." With a nod, he indicated the rocking chair that was normally his domain. I sat and watched as Cayuse Jem began to remove his outer garments. Instinctually, I blushed and turned away. This was a part of rustic life to which I was quite unaccustomed. I had never seen any other man before without his garments, and I did not reason it seemly to start now.

But Cayuse Jem would not let me escape so easily. I heard the soft splash of water as he entered the tub and then his familiar bark: "Boy," he said, and I found myself forced to face him. "Brush." He nodded toward an upper shelf, and I reached up to grab the brush and handed it to him. As I did, I saw through the clear water to all of him. There, in the water and out of his clothes, I was taken with the immensity of the man. As I noted before in this journal, Cayuse Jem is not fat, but he is large. Powerful. His chest and belly are swathed in the same thick russet hair that colored his beard, mounds of it. He took the brush from me, placed it into the water, and rubbed his hands against the thick bristles. I took my place again on the chair.

This time, I kept my face turned toward Cayuse Jem.

"Boy," he said again. "Soap." I retrieved the soap from another shelf and watched as Cayuse Jem began to bathe himself. I was uncomfortable, but I was not sure why. This was a private moment, but it was being shared between us as matter-of-factly as eating breakfast or falling asleep. I watched as Cayuse Jem soaped his limbs, his belly, and his nether parts. I watched as he doused his head in water and rinsed his thick beard. I felt as though I should speak, as though I should say something, but I did not know what to say.

So I said nothing.

"Boy," Cayuse Jem said again, holding out the brush with his hand. "Back." For a moment, I thought Cayuse Jem was indicating some type of direction rather than a part of the body, but then I understood. Without a word, I inched forward, knelt beside the metal tub, and hesitantly began to rub the thick bristles against the taut and knotted muscles of Cayuse Jem's shoulders.

"Harder," he said.

"Yes, sir," I replied, endeavoring to comply, but my efforts were not good enough.

"Harder, boy," Cayuse Jem said again, though his voice never wavered, nor raised in pitch nor volume. "That's a week of work you need to scrub off."

It was perhaps the longest sentence Cayuse Jem had thus far uttered to me. I scrubbed hard between the blades of his shoulders, as hard as my weary arms would allow. "Lower." In small circles I moved the brush as Cayuse Jem commanded. "Lower." My hand was now wholly submerged underwater, which I daresay I found somewhat soothing, though drops of perspiration beaded on my forehead. "Lower, boy," Cayuse Jem commanded in his even tone again, and though I feared I would need to scrub him halfway to perdition, I did as directed, moving the brush as far down as it would go.

My work seemed to have been met with approval, for Cayuse Jem grunted and suddenly stood, dripping water onto the floor, standing naked afore me.

"Towel." I rushed to fetch the patchy, threadbare towel Cayuse Jem kept near the wash basin next to his bed. I handed this to him, and he patted himself slowly.

As he stood afore me, I had an opportunity to see all of him. I knew I should not look, and I cannot wholly explain why I did so. The power that defined his torso and limbs also carried through to the rest of him, to his haunches and his loins. I had never seen another man this way before, and the sight of it...

I am unsure even why I am writing of this. It is unseemly to do so. Perhaps it was simply the shock of the moment.

When he finished drying himself, Cayuse Jem stepped out of the water. "Your turn."

At this I balked. "I—I do not think I need to bathe, sir," I said, unsure of why I was saying this. The water seemed quite soothing, and one deep inhalation was all the evidence required that a bath would do me good.

"Boy," Cayuse Jem said. There was no malice in the way he said the word, but I could hear the gravity in his voice. I looked at him. "Your turn."

I nodded.

I did not wish to disrobe in front of him. I cannot say as to why—Cayuse Jem was still unclothed in front of me—but I felt suddenly awkward and shy. I turned, facing away from him, and stripped myself of my garments as quickly as possible. I stepped into the water and began to soap myself, all without meeting Cayuse Jem's gaze. For his part, Cayuse Jem sat in the chair and watched me, though he made no attempt to clothe himself. It was still quite hot outside, despite the late hour, and I suspected the air evaporating off of Cayuse Jem's form was cooling. Still, to have him simply sit there, unclothed, was all a bit unnerving.

I bathed as hurriedly as I could, though I must admit the warmth of the water provided welcome solace to my tired muscles and limbs. Nonetheless, I quickly cleaned myself and moved to exit the tub when Cayuse Jem extended a hand for the brush.

I suppose I must have my back cleaned as well.

He rubbed my flesh rather vigorously—indeed, I was afraid he would rub it quite raw—but, to my surprise, it did not hurt at all. If anything, his exertions felt almost invigorating, though by this late point in the evening, utter exhaustion was truly taking root in me. When his task was complete, I closed my eyes and settled against the rapidly cooling metal once more, enjoying the almost-cold feeling surging through my body.

"Boy." I opened my eyes and found myself staring into the brown orbs of Cayuse Jem. I had imagined any individual with red hair would have green eyes, like the Irishmen I had seen in Boston, but the color of Cayuse Jem's eyes almost matched the shade of his hair.

"Boy," he said again, this time placing his large, warm hand on my thin, tired arm. He waited another moment, ensuring he had my full attention. "You've done good work this week, boy."

I blinked. I was not expecting this. I was not expecting any praise whatsoever, considering my utter incompetence in these realms of manual labor and the minor revolt I had attempted only yesterday. I felt a lump rise in my throat. "Thank you, sir," I managed to say.

Cayuse Jem nodded toward the anteroom. "Dry up and off to bed with you, boy," he said.

He handed me the towel, and I stood to dry. I felt suddenly less shy. "What about the tub, sir?" I asked.

"Dry up and off to bed with you, boy," he repeated, though—and I would not swear to this—I almost heard a smile in his voice. I nodded, patting myself dry and paddling my way to my small straw bed. As I lay down to sleep, I heard a grunt—and then watched through the doorframe as Cayuse Jem lifted the tub, water and all, and carried it out the door.

8 July 1888

MY FAMILY IS Lutheran, though we are not what one might term strictly observational. As a child, the other inhabitants of the region were so widespread and scattered that regular services were impractical, and my father was never one to believe any day—even Sunday—should be a day of rest. This is certainly true as well at Cayuse Jem's ranch, and thus my Sunday started as any other day of the week.

Perhaps it did not start quite the same as the others, for this morning I had my first lesson milking the old cow Cayuse Jem kept among the horses in the barn. It was early—barely the crack of dawn—when Cayuse Jem woke me and took me to the barn.

"Watch, boy," he said, taking a small three-legged stool and situating himself at her side. She was an old brown-and-white Jersey and seemed as sleepy as I did, almost absentmindedly munching on the straw Cayuse Jem had provided her. Cayuse Jem patted the old cow on her shoulder affectionately, saying low words of encouragement before bracing his shoulder against her side. Reaching underneath, he grabbed her udders, and after a moment's hesitation, thin streams of milk began to shoot into a metal pail.

"Your turn, boy," Cayuse Jem said, stepping up and off the stool and indicating with his hand that I should take his place. I stepped forward hesitantly; I confess I felt an apprehension over this task I had not felt with any of the others. I knew cows were docile creatures as a rule, but the sheer bulk of the animal was intimidating. "Never approach a cow from the back," Cayuse Jem was saying. "If they cannot see you, they may lash out and kick. Always approach from the front or side." I did not find the knowledge that cows were, in fact, predisposed to violence comforting. Nonetheless, I took my place on the stool and slowly began to reach for the udder.

"No," Cayuse Jem interrupted, halting my actions. "You can't just grab at her. She has to know you are there."

I was momentarily taken aback by his directions, unsure in their meaning. Then I remembered the way Cayuse Jem had patted the cow and spoken softly to her. I mimicked his actions, though my hand shook as I did so. "There, there," I said, "it will all be okay—" Here I drew a blank, not knowing by what moniker I should address the animal. "What is her name?" I asked Cayuse Jem.

His first response was a faint air of bemusement. "She doesn't have a name."

"Well, she should have a name," I said. I was stalling for time, trying to settle my nerves, and we both knew it. "Don't you think? She provides us with milk. She works hard to produce it. It seems only fitting the cow have a name."

"By all means," Cayuse Jem replied. "Name her."

It was a small puzzle, but one enough to distract my mind, and I was glad of it.

"Io," I finally said after a less-than-concise consideration. "She shall be called Io." I suspected it was hardly a usual name for a cow in these parts, though I thought it terribly fitting. I surmised that Cayuse Jem did not understand the name's derivation, though he did not ask me for an explanation, and thus I did not provide one.

"Io," he repeated, the name seeming odd on his tongue, though he proffered no objection. He said nothing else but nodded at the cow's mammary glands, and I resumed the task at hand.

Yet as I reached for the cow's udders, she moved, stepping forward. I presumed she was simply readjusting her stance in order to better consume her morning repast, and so I adjusted my stance as well. When I reached once again for her udders, though, she again moved, this time shifting back. For several moments we continued this dance, Io shifting her bulk forward or back or to the side, while I moved the stool and myself accordingly.

If this was a contest of intellect, it was clear I was being soundly routed by an animal that was hardly known for its sagacity.

Finally, and with no small sense of exasperation, I sighed and turned to Cayuse Jem. His look of bemusement had been replaced by an expression rife with amusement. "She knows you're scared."

Cayuse Jem's words failed to provide the type of concrete instruction I had been seeking. "And?"

As a response Cayuse Jem grabbed me firmly on the shoulder and roughly pushed me into Io's side. I would have imagined that the cow would retreat as a response, but to my surprise, she seemed almost comforted by the firm presence of my shoulder against her side. She pushed back against me, making the udders easier to reach.

But Cayuse Jem had not finished his lesson. Reaching below the cow, he positioned his right hand upon her udder; then he used his left to take my own hand and place it on top of his. I was cognizant first of the feel of his grip—powerful, strong, but solid, consistent, almost temperate and reassuring. Then I traced his fingers to understand their configuration upon the cow's mammary. Lastly, I placed my hand upon Cayuse Jem's own as he milked the cow, compressing and releasing his fingers in a rhythmic pattern that swiftly produced the desired outcome.

Cayuse Jem backed away, and I was left to confront the beast once more. I pushed my shoulder into her side firmly, and Io responded in kind. I placed my hands upon her mammary as instructed, and though it took a few attempts, I soon had a steady stream of milk emanating from the cow.

Something within the sensory nature of the experience caused my mind to reel back to a moment in my childhood when, age seven, my father taught me to shell a walnut. It was Christmastime, and walnuts were a favorite of mine, but my small, weak fingers could not manipulate the nutcracker, no matter how hard I tried. Growing impatient with me, my father reacted in the same manner as Cayuse Jem; taught me by showing me, by grabbing the tool and demonstrating how it should be done. I vividly recalled struggling with the nutcracker for several moments and—just as I was about to admit defeat—sweet victory, as I manipulated the device and my fingers in just the right manner to crack the nut and reach the highly prized meat inside. It proved, I supposed, what Archimedes always said about a lever and a pulley offsetting the weakness inherent to any man, but as a child I only thought of my excitement at having finally mastered the task. Yet as I turned triumphantly to show my father, he had already drifted away, his attention now focused on other matters. I half expected the same response from Cayuse Jem, to be absent when I demonstrated my triumph; but there he was, looking on with interest, watching as I filled the pail with milk. Then he clapped me on the shoulder and spoke but two words—"Good boy"—before spinning on his heel and walking out of the barn to begin his day's exertions.

I initially suspected that successfully learning to milk Io would have been the highlight of my day, but late in the afternoon, we also had visitors from the manor house. Most small farms in the territory are largely sustentative, supporting only those who dwell on their property. But my father had created a more cooperative structure with the farms on his land. Each produced primarily a single product, and those products were redistributed by men from the manor house—after my father had taken his share, of course, some for our use, and some for the market.

It was a reasonable system, ensuring that the success or failure of one farm could be buffeted by the work of others. It allowed my father the opportunity to employ a man like Cayuse Jem as a specialist—training the Appaloosa—in turn supplying him with foodstuffs and other items to supplement his needs and his work.

I was excited to see people from the manor house, even if the expedition turned out to be headed by Cheevers, who, as a rule, was as garrulous and voluble as Cayuse Jem. The chickens and Io provided eggs and milk, and there were bushes around the ranch to pick blackberries and gooseberries, but Cheevers brought salted pork and fresh beef, vegetables, cheese, fresh butter, bread, and coffee. All of these were duly unloaded and stored for our consumption.

Eagerly I asked Cheevers for news of the house, and though he had little to say, he did press a note in my hand: Dora. In her letter, my sister spoke lovingly to me and exhorted me to "keep my chin up," hoping that we would be reunited soon. And while she had been prevented by my father from forwarding to me any books, she did send along with her letter another precious commodity—a heaping portion of our cook's nut-and-date loaf. My favorite. That night, I cut myself a healthy slice of the loaf, and one for Cayuse Jem as well, and we ate them lavished with the butter Cheevers had brought and consumed with a large quaff of the milk that I, myself—me—had procured that very morning.

9 July 1888

BY GREAT HAPPENSTANCE Mr. Mackey, the peddler-man, came by today. I remember Mr. Mackey from when I was a youth, directing his overstuffed cart pulled by two gray amblers up the long, tree-covered walkway of my father's manor house. My sister Dora and I used to watch his approach with zealous anticipation, wondering what little treasures Mr. Mackey might bring our way. This time the peddler-man caught me rather unawares, as I was mucking the stalls when he thrust his head into the barn door. I was lost in deep thought, contemplating Cayuse Jem's expression as he watched me master the art of milking the cow. I was remembering, too, his words from this morning: "These eggs are just fine, boy." I had been trying rather diligently not to get shells into the eggs, and I remembered this time to butter the pan lavishly before putting them in. I had not yet mastered the trick of preserving the yolk, as I knew Cayuse Jem preferred, but it was evident my cooking had marginally improved, and I was secretly pleased Cayuse Jem had noted my efforts.

This is what I was thinking as I was cleaning the stalls, and so I did not hear the peddler-man approach.

"You, boy!" Mr. Mackey called out, interrupting my reverie. The timber of his voice reminded me instantly of the singsong manner in which he sold his wares when he came to the manor house, but here his merry tone was replaced by a curt, almost annoyed, bellow. "Boy!" he repeated. "Where is the owner of this fine establishment?"

He spoke as a man who disdained consorting with those he perceived to be of lesser worth. I knew that tone well; Abernathy, my father's lieutenant and sister's intended, spoke the same way, spoke to almost every man—save for my father, of course—as if he had discovered him on the underside of his shoe. Oh, yes, I knew that tone, and I did not like it one bit, not in Abernathy, nor in anyone, and certainly not the way I heard it voiced here, not in the way the peddler-man spoke to me, nor in what he had implied about Cayuse Jem. I have always abhorred snobbery, especially when, as in this case, it lacked the most trifling of foundations. So I gave him not the satisfaction of a reply. Instead, I set my jaw and answered the peddler-man with silence.

This only inflamed the man more. "Boy!" he spoke louder, as if the volume of his words was the source of the problem. He walked closer to me, spitting on the ground as he did. "You deaf, boy, or dumb, or what?" He spat again. "Where's the dull hick that owns this place, huh?"

Now he had done it. I straightened my spine, making myself as tall as possible, and cleared my throat before responding. "Good day to you, Mr. Mackey. I am hoping the heat of this morning has not taxed your journey too much. It seems a tad stifling to me, even for this time of the year. Don't you agree?" The cultured polish and erudite language in my response caught the peddler-man wholly unaware. I could tell by the taxed expression on his face that he knew something was not quite right with this scene—his mental processes were churning, trying to determine the source of such incongruity, trying to figure how a simple farmhand could speak with the polish of an educated man. I smiled at him. He was about to find out how correct his instincts were.

"Boy—I mean—have we met?" the peddler-man finally muttered.

"Of course we have met, Mr. Mackey," I replied, in my most counterfeitly gracious tone. I had him twisting now and was rather enjoying myself. "Naturally, it has been a few years since we last spoke. And the passage of time does change a young man so." I stuck out a hand in a seemingly friendly gesture. "Nathanial Goldsmith."

The peddler-man's hand was halfway to my own when the significance of my name became clear to him. "Nath— Young Master Goldsmith," he sputtered, doffing his hat in respect before taking my hand in an eager show of remonstration. "I—I did not recognize you."

"I should say not." The friendly pretense had left my voice, replaced with a tightly controlled anger that demonstrated to Mr. Mackey that he was not trifling with some common rustic after all. "I should imagine a man in your position—who makes a living by selling his wares to customers—would do his best to ingratiate himself with all manner of folk, so as to keep their custom."

"Of course, of course!" the flustered man stammered. He gripped his hat so tightly it bent in twain in his hands. "It—it is the heat, as you said, young master. It upsets my disposition so."

I smiled again, but my tight lips indicated the true veracity of my expression. "Then your manner is easily forgiven," I said. I took a step closer to Mr. Mackey. "But please be assured—Cayuse Jem works for my father, like so many of the good people in these parts. And I would suspect my father would prefer you treat them in the same manner as you treat him." I took another step closer and spoke with a low voice, to be sure I was understood. "Do you comprehend my meaning? Or should I communicate to my father that this particular route seems to be too— challenging for you and your amblers to capably service?"

"No, no—I mean, yes—I mean—what I mean to say, young sir, is there is absolutely no need to mention any of this to your father. Is there?" The man's concern for his livelihood was writ across his face. I smiled once more. My father, I felt quite certain, would demonstrate paltry interest in how Mr. Mackey treated Cayuse Jem or any of his clients, save for himself. But there was little need to acquaint Mr. Mackey with such a fact.

"Indeed," I said. "We shall then consider the matter settled." The peddler-man opened his mouth but, perhaps thinking the better of it, only nodded hastily in reply. "Now," I added, "if you would be so kind as to wait right here, I will see if Cayuse Jem has any need of your wares." And without another word, I slowly turned and walked, in a rather unhurried manner, out of the barn to look for Cayuse Jem.

Given the time of day, I would imagine Cayuse Jem to have been in the paddock, working with the horses. Yet I found him only a few steps outside the barn doors, stopping for a brief respite in the shade of the barn's wall. Had he heard what I had said? He made no indication, one way or the other, and demonstrated no other expression when I told him the peddler-man was here.

Cayuse Jem went with me to the peddler-man's wagon. I was amused to discover Mr. Mackey had indeed not moved one inch from whence I had left him. Cayuse Jem greeted Mr. Mackey with a curt nod. He took a handful of moments to look over the man's wares and made two or three small purchases, handing over a few coins before returning to his work. I, on the other hand, was not yet done with the traveling salesman. "And now, Mr. Mackey," I said, "what books do you have?"

Books were expensive items in the territory, and Mr. Mackey's eyes gleamed wide—happy, I would suspect, in learning he had not lost my custom after all. "I'm afraid I don't have quite the stock I used to carry," Mr. Mackey said, "on account of there being less call for books than before you left." As a child the advent of the peddler-man's cart always meant new books for me, and the clever salesman had learned to keep his tomes well stocked whenever he visited the manor house. "I wasn't quite expecting to find you here," he added, and I could tell he was wondering, for the first time, exactly what I *was* doing here. "Still, I am sure one or two of these volumes will prove to your satisfaction."

"I shall take them all."

"All?" The man had been rummaging around his wagon and had produced a dozen different tomes in all manner of size and scale. "Are you sure you want all of them, Young Master? I fear you will find many of the volumes—somewhat elementary, for a man of your abilities."

"All of them," I repeated. "Regardless of their contents, please."

Gleefully, the peddler-man complied. I confessed myself disappointed at the scant number of volumes in his custody, but was thankful he had at least some books in his possession. Asking the man for a scrap of paper, I hastily penned a quick note and handed it to him. "Take this message to the manor house and give it to Cheevers. He will see that you are compensated."

"Oh, yes, sir, young master, yes, I shall!"

"And Mr. Mackey?" The peddler-man had moved to depart but turned again to face me once more. "I just wish to reiterate that I shall, of course, say nothing of this affair to my father. I expect you shall like to do the same."

The peddler-man was no fool. "Of course, young master."

"Good. And in the meantime, should you find yourself coming back this way and have more books in your possession, I shall purchase all of them, as well."

"Very good, sir. Thank you, sir." And without another word, the peddler-man climbed back onto his wagon and departed on his way.

Normally the peddler-man might come through an area like this twice in one year, but I suspected I would see Mr. Mackey again before the summer was out. Hastily, I took my new treasures into the cabin and secured them next to my sleeping place. I longed for nothing more in the world than to begin reading them right away, but there was work to do. Moreover, I thought that the anticipation of the moment when I cracked the book's spine for the first time would hasten my work and make the day far lighter. And so it did, at least in my own heart. Indeed, I have even taken the time to write in my journal ere I set out to peruse my new riches. Still, anticipation can only add so much to one's zeal, and thus I think the time has come to set this diary aside for the night.

10 July 1888

THE BOOKS MR. Mackey sold me have proven a rather disparate lot. There is a spelling book of Mr. Webster's, plus one of his syllabaries—hardly anything I should need—an almanac, two bibles, and a recipe book by Mrs. Beeton. There are two books intended for child readers by Mr. Alger—though in my desperate situation I shall take what I can get—and a book by Mrs. Alcott for women. Then there is a book by Mr. Irving I have previously read but shall enjoy doing so again; a collection of humorous if somewhat ribald poems; and, to my great delight, selections from Shakespeare. There are no complete works, but there are passages from many, and I do not know of any better balm for my soul than the words of the great English Bard.

Though I confess this experience to not be as odious as I had anticipated. The work is hard; harder than anything I have ever before attempted, though as I previously indicated in these pages, I am no indolent soul. I am not sure if this is making me into a "man," as my father had directed, but I confess that I do not abhor my time here with Cayuse Jem. There is a simplicity to life on this little ranch; the feeling I have at the manor house, at my father's house, that feeling I somehow do not belong, that feeling of always being on tenterhooks... I do not have that feeling here. True, this is no library, no ivory tower—that is my true home, the place I always long to be. But being here... There is something about it that is...easing, perhaps? I am quite unsure how to articulate the feeling... Perhaps the charms of rustic living are simply wearing off on me. Or perhaps it feels less necessary to put on a façade and pretend to be the man my father longs me to be while I am here.

Or perhaps I am content because I finally have some books. It is good to be surrounded by friends once more.

Tomorrow, Cayuse Jem tells me, I am to begin working with the horses. I should hope working with the creatures themselves will be more engaging than working with their refuse.

11 July 1888

IT IS DIFFICULT to describe exactly what Cayuse Jem does with the horses, as I am unsure of what it is myself, and Cayuse Jem is hardly forthcoming on the matter, though our dialogue has expanded from the monosyllabic exchanges we first had upon my arrival here. He breeds the horses, though not in great quantities; he raises them; and he trains them in the particular movements of equestrian sport. This much I know. He also catches wild Appaloosa on occasion or works with those brought to him.

But he does not break them, as I understand the process to be performed elsewhere. He never uses the whip and never seems to lose his temper with the beasts. And I have noticed that he seems to approach each horse individually. One he chastises; one he coddles; another he coaxes and wheedles; still another he scampers with to and fro. It is a sight, to be sure, to see a large man like Cayuse Jem scamper with a colt, but I know of no other word to describe his activities.

Cayuse Jem explained that the best-trained horses would be shipped East for equestrian competitions and other such enterprises. Apparently, rich associates of my father will pay handsomely for a well-trained Appaloosa, since their dappled hides and black-and-white patches stood out starkly compared to the more common, single-hued varieties of horse found back East. I could understand the appeal. They were beautiful creatures to be sure. And they surely stood out amongst a crowd of similar creatures. Though I daresay that, the more I stared, the more I thought the Appaloosas looked quite like the zebras I saw at the zoo in Boston. Well, perhaps the Appaloosa are a bit more elegant in their form and disposition than a zebra; nonetheless, all the black-and-white seemed more appropriate for the wild savannahs of darkest Africa than a refined equestrian arena in Boston, New York, or Philadelphia.

Those horses that are not fit for the equestrian circuit, Cayuse Jem explained, are either returned to the wild or sold to a local farmer for field work. Judging by the tone in his voice, I suspected Cayuse Jem preferred the former outcome to the latter.

"Why is that?" I asked him, curious as to his thinking on the subject.

Cayuse Jem stroked his beard as he spoke. "There are work horses, racing horses, show horses, wild horses—all kinds of horses. These Appaloosa, well, they weren't made for working, not on a farm, pulling the plows and such, not like other kinds of horses. They just don't like it much."

"But you sell them for shows, yes?" I asked, needling the man a bit. "Do they like being dressed in fancy saddles and halters and paraded around an arena?"

Cayuse Jem gave me an appraising look. "As a matter of fact, boy, they do. Look at them. Just look at how they puff out their chests when they show. Trick riding, fancy walking—they like it all. The Nez Perce used to teach the Appaloosa all different manner of tricks, just to show off, as part of their different ceremonies. Oh yes, boy, these animals like to put on a bit of a show."

"I saw an equestrian show once in Boston," I said, "where one horse was so dolled up in resplendent finery one could not even see the animal underneath. And another had wings made of gossamer and ostrich feathers so large you would swear Pegasus had leapt forward from the pages of Bullfinch's mythology to stride across the arena."

Cayuse Jem gave a wry chuckle. "Well, it's true some folks back East don't got much sense, and rich folks have a might less, I would wager. It don't take fancy dress to make one of my horses show. Why, look at this, now, boy. You watching?" As he spoke, Cayuse Jem was entreating one of his horses to raise its foreleg at a perfect ninety-degree angle. I must confess it was somewhat enthralling to observe a grown man—especially one as Herculean as Cayuse Jem— endeavor to convince a horse to raise its forelimb just so. He was gentle with the beast, coaxing it, almost charming it, rewarding it with a bit of sugar or apple when it did as asked. For a good half hour I watched as Cayuse Jem patiently put the horse through its paces, and never once did he raise his voice or speak in an angry tone, even when the horse failed to learn what the large man wanted.

"Why not use the whip?" I asked. "Would the creature not learn quicker?"

"Quicker, perhaps, but never better," Cayuse Jem replied. "To train a horse like that is to make it afraid of you. That's no good for horses," he added. "You can't win a horse through fear. No, trust must be earned," he told me.

"Can an animal truly ever trust a man?" I asked. "One cannot speak to it, or assuage its concerns."

"Aye," Cayuse Jem replied, "and that is the only trust that truly matters."

Leaving his horse for a moment, Cayuse Jem turned his gaze toward me. "You must understand, boy, the nature of a thing," he said.

"The nature of a horse?" I asked.

"A horse. A man. A thing. Anything."

"And if I understand the nature of the beast, then what? Then I can change it?"

"You cannot change the nature of any creature," Cayuse Jem said.

"Then I can temper its behavior? Alter its condition?"

"You cannot change the nature of any creature," Cayuse Jem repeated.

I smiled. His logic was downright Augustinian, though the saint would exhort us to fight our inner natures, flawed as they must be. I had no sense Cayuse Jem felt the same as Saint Augustine.

"And so what, then?" I asked. "Why understand the nature of a thing if one cannot alter it?"

"So you may love it," Cayuse Jem plainly replied before turning back to his horses.

It was, I must say, a wholly unexpected response. And yet, I believe I understood what he meant. A horse for Cayuse Jem is like a book to me. For me, to read a book, to ponder it, to analyze it, is to understand its nature. When I peruse a white page with black lettering covering the vast majorities of its expanse, it asks of me—nay, begs me, demands of me—to understand its essence, its meaning. Its nature. Cayuse Jem must study his horses the way I do my books. I know I shall never feel for horses the way I do for books. I shall never feel for anything what I feel for books. But I can certainly respect Cayuse Jem, and I can understand his viewpoint, and the man himself, perhaps a shade more now.

12 July 1888

IT IS MILDLY unnerving to me to read over the words I have penned so far in this little journal of mine and uncover how many of my life's events worth recording since coming to work for Cayuse Jem have transpired in the stables—as if the central focus of my life has become the shoveling of excrement. And yet I must recount another, certainly an event that, if not the most noteworthy so far, triggered the greatest sensation at the time of its occurrence. I was working in the stables and contemplating Chaucer's first great tale, that of the Knight. In the story, the two boon companions—Palamon and Arcite—began a war because they both happed to fall in love with the same woman. On the eve of the final battle, both men prayed to the gods, Arcite to ask for victory and Palamon to ask for the hand of their beloved, Emelye. The gods granted both of their wishes; Arcite won the battle but subsequently forfeited his life, leaving Palamon alone to marry their love.

I was pondering this tale because it always struck me that Chaucer's concern in this little missive is the capricious nature in which the gods granted each man his deepest desire. Arcite was victorious but did not live to enjoy the spoils of war; and Palamon married his love but won her through default, losing perhaps his honor (and her admiration) in the process. While most scholars have focused on the end result of this entire process, I was actually curious about the prickly nature of the gods and how Chaucer's meaning might shed some light on my own current predicament. It is perhaps an old maxim—but a useful one—to be careful what one wishes for, but is Chaucer perhaps suggesting that the gods—whimsical and ill-behaved as they oft seem to be in these tales—seek to fulfill our deepest dreams and wishes, only to use them to destroy us? Is that the nature of higher beings, at least in Chaucer's time and Chaucer's mind? Should we not dream nor wish, to ensure the safety of our own selves? Do we ultimately pray for our own destruction?

This particular moment felt prescient because, as I was endeavoring to clear out a particularly sizeable and malodorous pile of horse manure, I was wishing—most intently—for deliverance from my current station, when I suddenly felt a presence behind me. The sensation was intently unnerving, as if I felt eyes upon me, studying me, inspecting me, long before I myself was cognizant of the presence of another human soul. I felt my skin erupt in goose-pimpled papules and shuddered as if some careless soul had just wandered across my own grave. I whirled around and saw that these sensations were not the product of any flight of fancy but that I was, indeed, being watched, and not just by anyone, but by a rather large, rather fearsome looking Nez Perce Indian. He was tall, well over six feet, with the long straight black hair indicative of his people. He wore no shirt, clad only in the buckskin pants commonplace amongst the Indians in this part of the territory during the summer months. His broad shoulders and developed musculature spoke to his power and his presence. Yet what was perhaps most unnerving was his face. It was utterly impassive, as blank as death, as the poet wrote, though the fact that I was mentally quoting Tennyson was the furthest thing from my mind in that particular moment of time.

I had been asking for deliverance from my toils, and here, I thought, was that deliverance, in the form of a gruesome death at the hands of this Indian brave. For a moment, I was as frozen as the vast polar wastelands of this world. But then my mind sprang to presence, and dropping the shovel, I ran from the barn to seek assistance from someone more capable—and of a more appropriate size—to deal with this unwelcome guest. Fortunately, I only had to travel a few yards before I collided with Cayuse Jem's barrel chest directly. Seeing the expression of horror on my face, the man held me in his powerful grip, endeavoring to calm my frantic mind. I attempted to explain the situation, but only a few babbling words escaped my mouth before Cayuse Jem spotted, across my shoulder, the interloper in the barn.

And yet if this new presence caused him any alarm, he did not show it. Instead Cayuse Jem walked over to the Indian man, extending his hand in greeting and exchanging a few low-slung words in the Indian's native tongue. The Indian greeted Cayuse Jem in kind, and it occurred to me— for the first time—that the Indian's presence here was not untoward or, indeed perhaps, not even unwelcome.

I felt my cheeks redden, that I had reacted in such haste and assumed that this stranger meant me ill intent. I desired nothing more than to beat a hasty retreat, but Cayuse Jem called me to him. "Boy." I came as bid, staring ashamedly at my feet. "This is our friend, Chuslum."

My manners and breeding overtook my unease over my previous behavior; I extended a hand and mumbled, "How do you do, sir?" I was still too embarrassed to look Chuslum in the face, but I was forced to when the Indian did not extend his hand to meet my own. It was only when I looked at him and saw the broad smile that had now crossed his features did he reach out and take my hand in his.

I smiled, too, though I still felt embarrassed at my reaction. "Chuslum provides me with horses sometimes, boy," Cayuse Jem explained to me, "and aids in my training. Now, we have some business to discuss," Cayuse Jem added. "So you best get back to work, boy."

"Yes, sir," I said, stooping to retrieve my shovel. "Nice to meet you, sir," I called to Chuslum as the two men walked out of the barn and into the light of day.

I watched as Cayuse Jem and Chuslum talked for several minutes, more than once noting one or the other gesticulated toward me. I felt my cheeks redden again. No doubt Cayuse Jem was embarrassed by my behavior. Had I acted in such a manner around my father and one of his colleagues, my father would brand me a coward and react most unpleasantly. I was ashamed by my lack of manly resolve. I determined to apologize to Cayuse Jem as soon as opportunity presented itself.

The conversation between the two men was brief, and I watched as Cayuse Jem and Chuslum crossed into the paddock with the horses. Palouse came to Cayuse Jem as usual, and the two men conversed for a few moments more before Chuslum mounted the horse and rode him out of the paddock, heading north, away from the small ranch.

I raised my eyebrows at this. The Nez Perce in this part of the territory were forbidden from owning or riding horses. Cayuse Jem saw the questioning look on my face but said nothing. I took my own moment, though, to speak up. "Sir, I wanted to apologize."

"Apologize? What for, boy?"

The words came out of me as a torrent. "I behaved atrociously just now, running from a man who was your guest. I should not have behaved so. I did not mean to—"

Cayuse Jem took both my arms in his hands and vigorously interrupted my speech. "You did exactly the right thing, boy, understand?" he said. I was taken aback by the forcefulness of his rejoinder, so I only nodded in reply. "If you ever think there is any danger, anything wrong, you come right to me. Is that clear?" I nodded again.

Satisfied by my response, Cayuse Jem dropped my arms. With a nod, he indicated the direction into which Chuslum and Palouse had disappeared. "Nez Perce needed to borrow an Appaloosa. Manhood ritual for one of the boys there. Just a little fancy riding. Palouse is up for it—he's done it before. They'll bring him back in a few days."

I wasn't quite sure what to say. "I did not think there was a reservation quite so close by, sir," I finally said.

"There isn't." Cayuse Jem held my gaze steadily. A small village, then. Perhaps just an encampment. Also quite illegal. "Is that going to be a problem, boy?"

I gripped the shovel tightly in my hands and prepared to resume my work. "I trust your judgment, sir. Implicitly," I added, offering Cayuse Jem a small smile before turning back to the task at hand.

16 July 1888

IT HAS BEEN several days since I have writ in my little journal. I have been injured and ill, and in need of convalescing. But I am well now, thanks to the kind ministrations of Cayuse Jem.

When I went to work with the horses it perhaps did not occur to Cayuse Jem to ascertain my level of previous experience with the creatures, or even if I was capable of riding one. It may not have occurred to the rancher that any individual raised in the territory cannot ride a horse, but four years in a bustling city dulled the sense of my horsemanship into a rather dismal state. Mounting a horse proved challenging enough; staying on one was clearly impossible.

I am unsure of what precisely happened next. I felt myself crushed against Cayuse Jem's chest, my face nestled against the thick russet of his beard. There was something comforting about the strength of his grip. The next thing I remember I awoke in his bed, with Cayuse Jem placing a damp, cool towel on my head.

"You've no broken bones," he said. His tone reflected his usual even, unhurried manner, but I thought I could detect more than a hint of worry in his voice. "I've checked."

"I'm sorry," I said. I didn't quite know why I said that, but I didn't know what else to say. I was embarrassed by my failures and my obvious weakness.

I felt sure Cayuse Jem would feel the same and be disgusted by my lack of even basic skill with the horse. But he betrayed no such emotion. "There's nothing to be sorry about, boy," Cayuse Jem muttered instead. "'It's my fault. I shouldn't have let you up there without making sure you were ready."

Cayuse Jem took the cloth to the wash basin, plunged it in deep, and wrung it dry before placing it back on my face. The cool relief it brought made me close my eyes.

"Stay awake now, boy," Cayuse Jem said, and I forced my eyes open once more. The lids felt heavy, though, too heavy to resist the spell of sleep. "No, stay awake, boy, stay awake!" Cayuse Jem said more forcefully, and I roused myself to attention. "You only blacked out for a minute or so, but that can be dangerous. You just need to stay up for an hour, to make sure you're okay. Then you can sleep. Hear me, boy?"

"Yes, sir," I mumbled.

"I'll stay with you."

"Will you read to me?" I weakly nodded my head toward the pile of books that lay in the corner of the room.

Cayuse Jem looked at the books warily. He took my hand in his great paws. "I think you need quiet now, boy," he said. I nodded, too weak and sore to argue any further.

For an hour Cayuse Jem tended to me, holding my hand and replacing the damp cloth numerous times. Every time I threatened to fall asleep he cajoled me to consciousness. "Stay awake for me, boy, come now," he would say. "Stay awake for Cayuse Jem." Finally, he seemed satisfied I was in no danger and let me sleep. He pulled the thin blanket up to my neck.

"Boy," he said softly to me, his face mere inches from mine. "I want you to know something." I opened my eyes wide one last time, looking into Cayuse Jem's russet-brown orbs. Such an unusual color for eyes. "Nat, I want you to know. I think you're a right good boy." And without another word he gently rubbed his palm on my face and turned and left the room. In less than a few seconds, I drifted off.

When I woke it was near dark, but Cayuse Jem was not in the house. I found water, bread, and cheese by the wash basin; I drank most of the former and ate little of the latter two. I wondered where Cayuse Jem might be, but I supposed my absence from the day's chores made more work for him. I felt bad about this and determined to do what I could to make it up to him. But taking even a few steps seemed to exhaust me, and almost against my will, I found myself back in bed.

I woke the next morning and the house was empty once more. I felt better than the previous day and got up to see Cayuse Jem riding a horse back toward the ranch. I prepared breakfast, so it would be ready for his return.

It took several minutes for Cayuse Jem to come to the house; judging from his wet hands and face, he had gone down to the stream to wash himself. "Why are you out of bed, boy?" he asked, though he quickly sat and devoured the eggs I had prepared, as hastily as if he had not seen a morsel of food pass his lips in over a day.

"I feel much better," I replied. "I am ready to resume my duties."

Cayuse Jem shook his head. "Nothing doing. You don't fool with hitting your head. You best take it easy today too."

I opened my mouth to argue, but one look from Cayuse Jem told me that any line of reasoning proffered on my part would be fruitless. Truthfully, I still felt a weary soreness in my bones and a throbbing dullness in my head, and another day of leisure might help the discomfort to abate.

Still, I did not waste my day entirely. When I felt up to it, I swept the floor of the shack, wiped down the table, and even used a damp cloth to clean the chairs and stove. I also picked up the book by Mrs. Beeton and began to read it. I had never before bothered to study the principles of cooking—I had always had servants for such work—but I realized that applying heat to transform the substance of an object was truly just a gastronomic extension of chemistry. While never my favorite subject in school, I had studied it quite extensively, and I was able to apply those scientific principles in preparing a dinner for Cayuse Jem. He had not asked me to do this, and breakfast was the only repast I had prepared so far, but thanks to Mrs. Beeton, and to Mr. Sinclair, the chemistry master at my old preparatory school, I managed to create a meal that was certainly tolerable, if not delicious.

Cayuse Jem seemed surprised by my efforts and, I hope, pleased. Mrs. Beeton spoke of "breaking down" the meat prior to cooking, and I realized that, through rough handling, the end result would be beef that proved more tender than what Cayuse Jem had previously prepared. I also learned that the proper application of heat was important. A fast sear would keep the meat moist and juicy.

There may be something to learn here, after all.

Cayuse Jem seemed satisfied by my efforts, but he was not pleased I had exerted myself. I had hoped to do more than write in my journal before bed, but he sent me off with no further argument. And though I attempted to return to my pile of straw in the floor, he would not hear of it, and once again I slept in his bed, and he on the floor.

17 July 1888

I HAVE DISCOVERED something about which I feel absolutely terrible.

The horse that bucked me bolted after I fell, breaking out of the paddock and damaging the fence in its flight. Though prompt action was required in order to secure the livestock, Cayuse Jem did not leave my side for more than an hour. As a result, several of the horses escaped, and it took Cayuse Jem all day and all night to track them down. And, ultimately, there were two he could not find, who disappeared completely.

This is all my fault. I have cost Cayuse Jem two valuable horses. I will have my father recompense him for his loss, but my gross incompetence caused these troubles.

What I do not understand is why Cayuse Jem would tend to me when his valuable livestock was in danger of escape. Or why he would not strike me for my incompetence, or at least shout. Indeed, I only discovered what troubles I had caused when I saw the makeshift repairs to the paddock fencing and realized two horses were missing. Only then did I discern what my failures had cost him. But Cayuse Jem never said a word to me.

I must make it up to him. Father will pay him for his loss, but I must make it up to Cayuse Jem as well. I simply must.

18 July 1888

I SPENT THE day walking around as if on eggshells. I still felt absolutely wretched over costing Cayuse Jem two of his horses and almost longed for him to strike at me or shout or anything to end my torment.

But, true to form, Cayuse Jem said nothing untoward to me the whole day long.

Finally, as we consumed our evening meal, I confessed to him I knew the troubles I had caused him. "I promise my father will pay you for the loss," I hurriedly added.

But Cayuse Jem shook his head. "It is of no concern to you, boy," he said.

I disagreed. "It was my fault, sir. Please. Let me make it right."

Cayuse Jem shook his head again. "The matter is closed, boy."

"But, sir—"

Cayuse Jem reached across the table and took my hand in his. His grip was firm and intent, though I felt no malice in his hands, nor in his words. "Boy, I have spoken on the matter. It is closed. Do you understand?" After a moment's hesitation, I nodded.

Cayuse Jem did not let go of my hand but clutched it ever harder as he continued to speak. "Boy, Nat, the fact that you feel the way you do lets me know you won't make the same mistake again. You've learned. That's all I ask of you, boy."

I nodded once more. "Yes, sir."

Cayuse Jem and I sat like that for a moment longer, with him holding my hand.

I still felt terrible over what I had done.

But I felt better as well.

19 July 1888

I SAW CHUSLUM today, returning Palouse to the paddock. He also brought with him a stricken deer, still wholly intact. I hoped Cayuse Jem would not expect me to dress the animal—Mrs. Beeton may offer useful guidelines for cooking, but I felt quite certain she had little to say about the proper preparation of a carcass as large as a deer.

I nodded at Chuslum and smiled, and the Indian greeted me in his turn. The unpleasant incident of the other day seemed largely forgot, though he still scrutinized me with those same careful eyes—as if appraising me, as if wondering my worth. I shook my head. Really, I must learn to surmount these petty prejudices.

Unlike the other day, Chuslum did not seem to be in any hurry, and he and Cayuse Jem fell into a deep conversation that lasted nearly half an hour. I was curious as to what they could be discussing, since the longest conversation I had managed to maintain with Cayuse Jem had lasted approximately two minutes, and Chuslum seemed a man whose tongue was cut from the same cloth as Cayuse Jem's.

As he prepared to leave, Chuslum came up to me and spoke a few words in his native tongue. "He is asking if you have recovered from your injuries," Cayuse Jem translated for me.

"I am much better, thank you," I said to Chuslum. "It is kind of you to ask after me." The Indian did not apparently need my response translated, as he nodded at me once more before silently heading away from the ranch and toward the wood north of the paddock.

"Sir," I said to Cayuse Jem, "how did Chuslum know of my convalescence?"

"When I was out looking for the horses, I found myself heading toward the Nez Perce encampment. Came across Chuslum making his way here with one of my mares. He found it near the Indian village. I asked him to bring it to the paddock and to check on you when he did." Cayuse Jem looked me in the eye. "He told me your face felt cool to the touch and that you were sleeping deep. That was mighty comforting to me."

"I see." I looked to where the Indian man had left us and watched as his form receded into the forest. I felt a small lump rise in my throat. "That was very kind of him," I said. Indeed, I found myself quite moved by Chuslum's simple, humane gesture.

Still, my brief reverie was disquieted by the dark expression that clouded Cayuse Jem's countenance. "Is something wrong, sir?"

Cayuse Jem paused, as if hesitating to respond to my query, before finally deciding to reply. "The Indians might have to move their encampment—again. They've barely settled there a year and a half. It's not right. They're not bothering anyone. Not out there."

"Why would they have to move, sir?" I asked. "As you say, they do not seem to be near to any farm or village. And if Chuslum is any indication, they seem a good and kindly people."

Even underneath his bushy beard, I could see the tension in Cayuse Jem's jaw. "Land used to belong to the government. Just a little slip of a valley between two hills. Weren't really good for much anything, so the government never cared much how it was used. But not anymore." He turned to look at me. "The new landowner wants them gone." He paused. "It could turn nasty before it's all done." With that, Cayuse Jem left me alone, grabbing a saddle from the barn before heading back to the paddock.

I stood in the yard for another moment, silently staring after the spot in the forest where Chuslum had just disappeared. I had no need to ask Cayuse Jem who the new landowner must be.

I already knew.

22 July 1888

BETWEEN MY WORK and my books, I have had precious little time to write in this journal.

I am also now taking lessons—lessons in horsemanship, that is. Cayuse Jem is teaching me as if I were a rank beginner—a wise precaution, to be sure.

He has proven to be a tolerant teacher. Even with wholly fundamental aspects of learning—such as how to approach the horse—Cayuse Jem has been patient with me. Of course, patience is something of a hallmark for the man. I readily see that now.

When I first met Cayuse Jem, I was struck by how similar he was to my father. But I realize now that impression was utterly without merit. Father is a bully, one who asserts himself unto people and situations. Cayuse Jem has all of Father's strength but none of his brutality.

To watch Cayuse Jem with his Appaloosas is to understand all, I believe. He does not bend the creatures to his will. He coaxes them. The distinction is subtle, and yet it makes all the difference in the world. Even less than their methods, though, is their motivation. My father seeks to break and bend in order to mold the world in his own image, to control it. That is what he wishes of me—to control me. But Cayuse Jem does not seek to make the world into anything it is not. This I know.

Of course, precisely what he does seek, at least with me, I cannot say.

23 July 1888

I WAS READING last night—Shakespeare—and Cayuse Jem asked me to read aloud from the book. This surprised me, as he had made no similar request before, but I happily complied.

I read a few of my more cherished passages; Hamlet, of course, and Benedick's comic, blustering speech about marriage. But the histories were always my favorite, and I ended with Prince Hal's speech from *Henry IV*, one I knew well enough by heart:

I know you all, and will awhile uphold
The unyoked humour of your idleness:
Yet herein will I imitate the sun,
Who doth permit the base contagious clouds
To smother up his beauty from the world,
That, when he please again to be himself,
Being wanted, he may be more wonder'd at,
By breaking through the foul and ugly mists
Of vapours that did seem to strangle him.
So, when this loose behavior I throw off
And pay the debt I never promised,
My reformation, glittering o'er my fault,
Shall show more goodly and attract more eyes
Than that which hath no foil to set it off.

When I had finished, Cayuse Jem sat silent and stared straight ahead, stroking his beard absentmindedly, his eyes closed in contemplation. Finally, he opened them. "And what does that mean, boy?"

I did my best to explain. "It's about a young man—a prince, but not one who was born to be a prince. And he must live his life in order to both please his father and to redeem him as well—to 'pay the debt' he never promised."

"And how does he do that?"

I smiled. This was the sort of conversation I thrilled to have in the hallowed halls of Harvard, and here I was experiencing the same type of discourse on a small ranch in the Idaho territory. "He does it by destroying himself completely, by becoming someone else."

Cayuse Jem stroked his beard some more. "So this is a sad story, then, boy?"

The ranchman's question surprised me, and I was unsure how to reply. "What do you mean, sir?" I asked.

Cayuse Jem leaned forward in his rocking chair and placed one of his brawny hands on my shoulder. "To live your life for someone else...to live your life *as* someone else... That's a sad thing, don't you think, boy?"

I felt a lump rise in my throat at Cayuse Jem's question. I am not sure I ever thought of this play in that particular way. I had always considered Prince Hal the clever one, the man who redeems the foul act of his father's usurpation of the throne and unites the kingdom, at least for a time. I had always believed he needed to deny his own self in what he had done, that it was imperative to the cause. I had never truly considered what that act had cost him.

I found myself incapable of voicing a response to Cayuse Jem's inquiry. So I only nodded in reply and then turned my face away from his.

Cayuse Jem held my shoulder in his hand for one moment more, then let go and leaned back once again in his chair. "Boy," he said, "can you teach me to read works like this?"

I turned my countenance once more, this time to look Cayuse Jem in the eye. And I nodded once more too. "Yes, sir."

26 July 1888

I DO NOT remember learning how to read. From my perspective, it was simply an act I was always able to do. What is so natural to me, what I can perform without any conscious thought into how I make the effort, is clearly more difficult for an individual, like Cayuse Jem, who had never determined to even start such an undertaking before.

Fortunately, I have the spelling book and syllabary from Mr. Webster. They shall prove to be useful tools in this endeavor. And I have the example of Cayuse Jem himself. As he teaches me horsemanship, how to ride and care for a horse, he is ever patient, never prone to frustration or anger. I shall endeavor to model my efforts on him as I teach the man how to read.

Our first forays into reading proved to be utterly disastrous. I knew enough to start with the alphabet, but I did not know the proper manner in which to present it to Cayuse Jem. It was as if I could show him the tools, but not how to use them. But then I hit upon the notion to associate each symbol with its corresponding sound, and to endeavor to ground Cayuse Jem in the phonology of the language first. Cayuse Jem is a capable speaker of English (when he deigns to speak at all, of course), and so this has proven a successful way to embark on this new adventure.

31 July 1888

BETWEEN MY HORSEMANSHIP lessons and Cayuse Jem's reading lessons, I have had precious little time for this journal. No matter. I feel my time is better spent with Cayuse Jem, teaching him, and learning from him as well.

4 August 1888

ONE THING I have learned during the past month or so I have worked both alongside and for Cayuse Jem is that—and really, not unlike school—there are few disruptions to the rather natural rhythms of life that develop from the toil necessary to maintain the ranch. At university, I would arise each morning at the same time, complete my morning *toilette*, attend breakfast and chapel, and then speed off to morning class, followed by luncheon and then more class and physical exercise before dinner and an evening of study and recitation. Of course, the individual nature of each class would alter on any particular day, and weekends differed to an extent, but I remember that any particular disruption to our schedule—a school holiday, or some special musical or theatrical performance in the evening—was acutely galvanizing to the spirit.

On the ranch, our labors are even more customary and regular, to the point that, even though I have been here a shade longer than a month, I feel as though I could move through my life by rote. I no longer resent the work I do for Cayuse Jem, nor the time I am spending with him—indeed, I have come to see much value in the man himself, if not wholly in the work I must perform while under his tutelage—but I must confess there is a certain tedium to the passage of time here itself. I suspect, if pressed, Cayuse Jem might even agree with me. It is not that the work lacks value or even that it is not, in some manner, beneficial, it is just—prone to monotony.

That is why, when Cayuse Jem told me over our morning eggs that I was to eschew my usual chores in favor of a different task, I found my heart quicken and a small thrill of excitement course through me.

"What am I to do, sir?" I asked.

Cayuse Jem gave me an appraising look. "You seem to be fancying your abilities as a cook lately, boy."

"Any tribute should go to Mrs. Beeton, sir, and not to me."

Cayuse Jem's appraising look turned into a smile. "Nonetheless, boy, we will be having guests for luncheon today. And I expect you to do your best."

Luncheon guests! "Might I inquire as to who is coming, sir?"

"Does it matter, boy?" Cayuse Jem asked me. "Will your efforts be any greater or lesser depending upon the company?"

"No, sir, of course not," I replied. "I was merely—curious—as to who we might expect."

"They are our guests. And there will be two of them. And I am sure they will be mighty hungry." And with that Cayuse Jem stood from the table and left the small house to begin his daily chores.

A luncheon! My mind coursed with the possibilities of who might be attending. Could my father be one of the guests? My initially giddy impulse turned to a more disquieting pose. My father would not be pleased to see me as a cook. While working with horses is man's labor, cooking is woman's work. No, my emergent abilities as a cook would not make him proud at all.

I began to feel a knot form in my stomach. Cayuse Jem would not subject me to such humiliations, would he? And then it dawned on me—no, I do not believe he would do that.

Cayuse Jem is not the sort of man to make sport of another's feelings. If my assessment of the man's character was correct, that would mean our guests would be someone else, and not my father.

Dora, perhaps? My sister would be amused by my abilities in the kitchen, and I would take great comfort in spending time with her. But who would the other guest be? Cheevers? And how would Cayuse Jem come to invite my sister in the first place? No. I needed to remove such considerations from my mind. Cayuse Jem had asked me to prepare the best meal I could. And so that is what I set out to do.

In the manor house, our meals were served in courses: hors d'oeuvres, soup, fish, the main, dessert, and cheese, with everything done as *service à la russe*. While I dared not believe that my newly won skills leant themselves to the preparation of so many dishes, at university our evening repast was generally served in three stages: soup, main course, and dessert. It might be too ambitious, but I thought—in the time I had–I could prepare all three and pull off something comparable.

The soup course was easy. We had some fine leeks in the root cellar that had come from the manor house a few weeks back. As Mrs. Beeton directed, I had been saving all vegetal refuse for the making of stock. Within minutes I had a large pot of water boiling away on the fire.

Cayuse Jem had prepared the venison Chuslum had brought as compensation for his use of Palouse. Mrs. Beeton had a recipe for venison steaks that were served with a bramble sauce. We had almost all of the ingredients, and I felt quite confident I could substitute some milk fat for sour cream.

The main course needed a side. We had some wild rice, which Cayuse Jem often placed in stews, but the rice on its own seemed plain. Mrs. Beeton had a recipe for rice croquettes, and we had stale bread I could turn into crumb. It seemed manageable.

Dessert. This was the course that filled me with dread. I never had much of a sweet tooth myself, and as a consequence, I had not even consumed a good many desserts, let alone prepared one. And a meal such as this demanded a cake or a pie. I had naught of the ingredients I would need for a cake, nor a way to prepare it, but Mrs. Beeton has a recipe for pie crust she called "foolproof," and I had a quantity of gooseberries on hand. Pie it would have to be.

I set out to organize my meal preparations. I confessed myself stimulated at the thought of preparing such a meal—daunting as it may be—and believed that this type of toil would be far less taxing than my usual work mucking out the stalls and toting water for the animals. I was never more mistaken in my life! I am unsure if it was the mounting heat of the day, the constant fire from cooking these various dishes, or the pressure of creating a meal that would be pleasing to Cayuse Jem and our mysterious guests, but my brow never ceased to be covered in sweat all morning. Furthermore, all that could go wrong, did: the stock pot boiled over, filling the small house with foul-smelling steam; the bramble sauce rendered too long, and the end result was far too thick to be labeled a "sauce;" and the croquettes ultimately resembled less the perfect spheres depicted in Mrs. Beeton's book and more misshapen rocks pulled from an igneous formation underneath a burning volcano. Plus, I daresay that Mrs. Beeton's description of her pie crust as "foolproof" had not before been tested by a fool such as I. I sighed. A meal like this would certainly not please my father. How would Cayuse Jem react?

I had barely time to clean up the kitchen refuse, set the table, and make our small house presentable when our guests arrived. Happily, there was no one from the manor house present at all, but rather Chuslum and another Indian, a youth whose years on this earth seemed to match my own. I exhaled deeply. Some of my earlier unrest subsided. Chuslum was a friend, and this youth—whoever he may be—certainly seemed friendly enough, if the wide smile on his face was any indication of his general temperament and disposition.

"Motsqueh," he said to me, holding out his hand in a near-exact imitation of a handshake. I took his hand, and he did indeed shake it, rather vigorously, and his enthusiasm and grin were so infectious that, despite my nerves, I found myself laughing as well.

I took the word he bandied about to me to be his name, and, indeed, it seemed to be the case. Standing next to Chuslum, the two were a striking if unusual pair. Chuslum was tall, broad-shouldered, with long dark hair and a rather stern countenance. Motsqueh, by comparison, was slight and lean, almost my identical in height and physicality. Unlike his companion, he cropped his hair short, though it maintained a wild, unkempt appearance.

They were dressed identically, their bare chests exposed, their skin the familiar, copper-colored hue innate to their peoples. They made a rather handsome pair. Father and son, I wondered? Though Chuslum seemed to admonish Motsqueh sternly once or twice for his excited tomfoolery, judging by the expression on his face, the muscular Indian seemed to be more amused than anything. It was evident how fondly he regarded the boy. Was that how fathers regarded their sons normally? My father had never looked at me in any similar capacity, but I did not suppose the Goldsmith family was typical in that regard, or any other.

I bade our guests as welcome as I could and invited them to sit. Cayuse Jem only had two chairs suitable for dining, which were reserved for our guests. I sat Cayuse Jem in his rocking chair, and had brought a stool in from the barn for myself. I served the first course, doing my best to explain the meal as Mrs. Beeton suggested. "This is a leek soup, made from vegetable stock and enhanced with some milk fat. I also cooked some small bits of pork fat until they rendered and purified, which Mrs. Beeton recommends adding to potato soup, but which I thought might also do well here." I paused, allowing Cayuse Jem to translate my words, noticing that my detailed description of ingredients and cooking techniques was translated to our guests in a monosyllabic reply I could only imagine was the Nez Perce word for "soup." Taking the stock of the room, I gave up any more description and took my spoon in my hand. I noticed, however, that our guests had already placed their bowls to their lips and were drinking their soup directly from the vessel. Eyeing me, Cayuse Jem did the same, and I followed suit. I supposed it would not quite do to expect refined manners among such rustic individuals, and I supposed as well Mrs. Beeton would not mind, at least not this once.

The soup was quickly drunk, and I hastily cleared the bowls and prepared our main course. This proved a bit more problematic for our guests, since—as I later learned—Indians were not accustomed to dining with silverware and had nothing resembling a fork at all in their culinary realms. Still, a venison medallion covered in bramble sauce was not something that could be consumed with one's fingers—at least not neatly. I saw Motsqueh staring at his plate in great puzzlement, so I took up the fork and knife in my hands and attempted to demonstrate the proper procedure for cutting meat. I exaggerated a sawing motion and deftly maneuvered the knife and fork until I had a small piece of meat on the end of my tines. Then I carefully used the knife to allocate a small amount of the sauce onto the meat. Finally, bringing the fork to my mouth, I served myself the meat.

My demonstration proved somewhat successful. Motsqueh clutched his fork as if he were performing farm labors and hacked at the meat with altogether too much vim and vigor. Breaking off a far-too-large chunk of meat, he stabbed it with his fork and slashed it through the sauce, bringing the entire morsel to his mouth and nearly swallowing it whole. I was thankful the meat was quite tender, and the youth's smile and happy nod indicated he found it to his liking.

We were an odd foursome, to say the least—the large-bellied mountain man, the two bare-chested Indians, and the son of Jessum Goldsmith. We could not maintain a conversation—since we did not all speak the same language, and since Cayuse Jem was, as translator, less than voluble—and to be perfectly honest, I am unsure what the four of us might have to discourse about, anyway. And yet, despite all this, we proved to be a rather jovial party. Cayuse Jem and Chuslum talked together in low tones, while Motsqueh did his best to communicate with me through gestures and sounds. He seemed utterly fascinated by the paleness of my skin, touching my face several times before a sharp word from Chuslum averted that behavior. I surmised he had little experience or contact with white people, and that some of our customs and ways might seem strange to him. Occasionally he would point to something in the room, as if to inquire to its purpose, and I would do my best to pantomime a response. It was all rather amusing, though it also presented me with a rather unique perspective on my own situation. Coming to Cayuse Jem's house had, initially, seemed to me as if I had stepped back in time, to a simpler, more rustic existence. And yet, I imagined that, for Motsqueh, this humble domicile was so different from his own life experience that it seemed as if moving forward in time. I pondered for a moment what Motsqueh might imagine if he could see the manor house, with all its finery and gas lights and indoor plumbing. I envisioned such an experience would be very enjoyable for me, and endlessly fascinating to Motsqueh as well, though I also imagined my father would be less than amused. When he directed me to understand the people of the territory, I somehow doubted he meant these people, even if they were here long before white men ever settled any of the lands west of the Dakotas.

Thoughts of my father made me think of the conflict between the Indians and his men over their presence on his land. Perhaps I could intervene somehow on their behalf. But I pushed such thoughts from my mind as I stood from the table to clear the plates and prepare dessert.

I was most unsure about dessert. The innards of the pie were quite fine—they were simply gooseberries boiled with sugar and a little flour to thicken their consistency. The crust, on the other hand... I placed the pie upon the table and took the plates to the small basin. Cayuse Jem had but four plates (and that was being generous, as one was clearly more a serving platter of some stripe, and the other a carving board for bread—it turned out beneficent the bramble sauce had proven so thick, after all). Thus I would need to rinse the plates and wash them before dessert. And yet I had barely immersed the first plate into the water when the temptation of a sweet treat proved too much for Motsqueh. Ignoring any sort of decorum or protocol he reached over to the pie, slid his fingers under the rim of the crust, and extricated a rather large hunk of the dessert for himself.

I had envisioned neat slices served with a thin sauce of cream I had prepared, my own version of the clotted cream I remembered fondly from teahouses in Boston. Instead I saw my pie with a rather sizable, hand-shaped hole in one side. Motsqueh's enjoyment of the dessert was evident, as he laughingly took a large bite, but his action drew a sharp retort from Chuslum. It pained me to see the lad's countenance darken, so ignoring the dishes I sat back at the table and, in perfect imitation of Motsqueh, I took a portion of the pie for myself with my own hand—smaller than the one Motsqueh had appropriated, but in the same crude manner.

I could tell Cayuse Jem was both pleased and amused by my action, and though Chuslum still seemed somewhat cross, the two older men followed suit. Soon, our bellies were filled with pie and a meal that, if I do say so myself, was surprisingly palatable.

Our dinner guests were more charitable in their appraisal of my culinary endeavors. Chuslum said, through Cayuse Jem, that the meal was delicious, and Motsqueh provided an animated lecture of such length and movement, punctuated with numerous excited hand and facial gestures, that I felt as though I relived the experience of eating it a second time, even if I could not understand the exact words he spoke. "Was it really adequate, sir?" I asked Cayuse Jem.

In reply, Cayuse Jem placed his large hand on my forearm. "Boy," he began, "that was the best meal I ever ate."

My eyes moistened; I was not expecting such high praise. "Really, sir?" I whispered.

Cayuse Jem leaned back in his chair, a satisfied hand resting on his belly. "I think," he said, "such hard work deserves a reward. I think these boys deserve a little holiday. Don't you?" Turning to Chuslum he translated his idea, and the tall Indian nodded his assent.

"But, sir," I said. "I have to clean up the dishes and then the afternoon chores—"

"Forget that," Cayuse Jem interrupted. "Go with Motsqueh. Have fun. Be back by sundown."

My new companion needed no explanation for what was said; eagerly grabbing me by the hand, he alit from his chair and dashed through the door, taking me north into the woods. Clearly Motsqueh had some specific destination in mind, but where we were headed, I could not say.

I admit to being apprehensive about going into the woods. I had been with Cayuse Jem for over a month, and yet, I had only ventured to the edge of the forest that bordered his land to pick blackberries and gooseberries on the bushes and trees that grew there. Going any deeper within seemed foolish to me, as I feared I might get lost, or worried that I might encounter a ferocious creature, a bear or a wolf. But Motsqueh moved through the forest as an eel moved through water, his lithe form slipping past branches and under tree limbs as if they were not present in the first place. It was difficult keeping up with him, and I was struck in the face more than once with an errant set of branches and leaves. Finally, my protests had their desired effect, and Motsqueh lessened his pace.

Treading more steadily now, Motsqueh took my hand once more to lead me through this thicker part of the woods. I found this rather over-friendly act somewhat confusing. Once or twice at preparatory school, and occasionally at university, I saw fellows everyone knew to be the best of friends do the same thing. The gesture belied a closeness between the two that, to me, was simply unknowable. Motsqueh and I were clearly no such boon companions, which is why I found his behavior decidedly off. We had barely just met. Perhaps it was simply a part of Indian culture.

As we walked, a small brown creature skittered across our path, and Motsqueh excitedly pointed at the animal and started repeating his name: "Motsqueh! Motsqueh!" It took me a moment to glean his meaning, but then I remembered that many Indian names also meant something else as words. I smiled at my new companion. "Do you mean to tell me you have been named for a chipmunk?" I asked him.

Motsqueh looked at me quizzically and then smiled. "Chipmunk," he said, the odd-sounding word rolling off his tongue with a laugh. I laughed as well. It was difficult to imagine a moniker more fitting, given the frantic energy and sweet disposition of the youth before me.

"Say," I said to Motsqueh, "what does Chuslum mean in your language?" Again, our difficulties in communication shone through, as Motsqueh only looked at me helplessly. I pondered how to convey my meaning. "Motsqueh," I said, pointing after the chipmunk. "Chuslum?" I asked, making what I hoped was a universal symbol for a question by shrugging my shoulders and upturning my hands.

"Ahh!" Motsqueh said, understanding my request. He scrunched his face for a moment in thought and then placed two fingers atop his head. Making a snorting sound, he stamped at the ground and pretended to charge at me. We both laughed. "A bull? Chuslum is named for the bull? Yes? Quite fitting, indeed," I said, noting with some satisfaction that Chuslum's moniker so neatly fit him as well.

Motsqueh pointed at me. "Nat?" he asked, querying as to the meaning behind my own name.

I was unsure how to pantomime the Hebrew connotation of "Nathanial," meaning "given by God," and considering the straightforward, earthly meanings to the Indians' names, I was frankly embarrassed to do so. So I improvised. "Nat" sounds just like "gnat," and so I mimicked the hum of a small buzzing fly, pushing my thumb and forefinger together in such a manner as to imitate a pesky insect, circling them near Motsqueh's head in a less-than-perfect imitation of an actual gnat. "Tiptip?" Motsqueh pointed at me. "Tiptip," he repeated, an incredulous appearance spreading across his raised brows and face, perhaps wondering what I had in common with an insect.

Motsqueh smiled once more. "Tiptip," he said for a third time, and I suspected I had just been accorded a new nickname, whether I was fond of it or not. Before I could utter any form of protest, Motsqueh grabbed my hand and dashed off again. This time we had not far to go, as we were soon to reach our destination.

I could see a clearing in the woods up ahead, and through the clearing, a small but deep pond. Clearly fed by underground streams, the waters were green and inviting. It was soon evident why Motsqueh had brought me here. Shucking his buckskin pants, the now-naked youth began to splash into the water, exhorting me with hand gestures and words to join him in the pond.

His nudity startled me, and I endeavored not to glance at any parts modesty suggests should remain covered. Instead, I removed my shoes, rolled up my pants, and slipped my feet into the water.

The coolness of the damp was the first sensation to overtake me, a welcome respite after a hot day cooking at the stove and a warm trek through the forest. The pool lacked the warm stagnancy of a still pond, which confirmed my suspicions it must be fed by underground streams.

Motsqueh was busy splashing around, diving under the water wholly before surfacing again in a completely different spot. And yet, seeing he was still alone in the pool, he came splashing toward me, emerging from the water and revealing once again his naked form to me. Blushing, I averted my eyes, as best I could.

If Motsqueh noticed the reddening of my cheeks, he made no indication. Instead the youth was clearly intent on me joining him in splashing about in the pool. "No, thank you, no," I said, waving my hands at him. But Motsqueh would not be deterred. He grabbed me by the arm with an impish grin and endeavored to drag me into the pool. "I said I cannot!" My response was, perhaps, more violent than I intended, lashing out with a sense of urgent fear as I steadfastly refused to enter the pool. Motsqueh dropped my arm, and his entire countenance was a question mark, wondering what he had done so acutely wrong. I felt ill at ease for having caused him such grief. "I—I cannot swim," I said to him, but my words meant nothing to him. "I do not know how to swim," I repeated louder, before finally doing my best to pantomime swimming while shaking my head wildly in an aggressive, back-and-forth manner.

Motsqueh finally seemed to understand what I was endeavoring to convey to him. He sat back for a moment in the water, and I confess myself thankful his nakedness was momentarily covered. Then Motsqueh started to imitate swimming motions again, only this time in a more controlled fashion, while also pointing at me. I understood.

He wanted to teach me to swim.

I had never really wanted to learn to swim before. For most of the year, it was simply too cold to swim in Idaho or Boston. During the summer months, as a youth, my father would have viewed such activity as foolish, and there were precious few places to swim around the manor house anyway. Indeed, I was not sure if we were on my father's land now, or if we had wandered onto someone else's property. During the summer holidays at school, I was generally left alone, with only a matron or master to look after me. Those days were spent in study. Any outings were to museums or other places of culture. There was no time nor occasion for seaside visits.

Now, though, the heat of the day, and of my earlier endeavors, made the pool before me seem cool and inviting. Still, I was scared. Motsqueh was not strong nor steady like Cayuse Jem or Chuslum (for a moment I imagined the two of them here, naked, swimming with us, though I swiftly pushed that image out of my mind). Nor was he as serious. But he did look to be completely earnest for the moment; he had stopped splashing about and instead offered me a steady hand and his most encouraging smile.

I looked into the waters of the pool again. They did not seem that deep; perhaps... I gave in. I removed my feet from the cool water and stood on the side of the grassy bank. I looked around, reassuring myself there would be no one to see me disrobe, though, indeed, it felt as if we were truly alone, the only two people for miles around. I removed my shirt, my breeches, and then, with shaking fingers, my underclothing. Taking Motsqueh's hand, I stepped farther into the pool.

My insecurity over the naked conditions of our bodies was replaced with the cold terror of stepping into such utterly foreign terrain. The liquid surrounding me provided no comfort or support, only the promise of murky nether realms. My feet slipped softly into the silty bottom, and I imagined sinking ever deeper, to my waist, my neck, and then to a watery grave. But these were simply foolish fears, and I knew I had to overcome them. I took a deep breath. Then another. And then, for good measure, I took one more.

Motsqueh was as patient as the hours, as patient as time itself. This was perhaps most surprising, since stillness was not a condition of which I considered him capable. As a teacher, though, he proved as steady as Cayuse Jem. He showed me how to move my hands, and how to paddle my feet. Then he motioned me to lie supine on my back, and allowed me to float in the water, keeping his arms underneath my back and waist at all times. Anxious as I was, I also found this activity surprisingly peaceful. Finally, he deemed me ready. Turning me over on my stomach, Motsqueh wrapped his arms around my waist and signaled for me to kick my legs and paddle my arms. The first few attempts ended with me imbibing some small quantities of water, but every time I faltered, Motsqueh was there to lift me. Finally, ungainly as I must have appeared, I managed to approximate the actions Motsqueh had described, and I was swimming.

I was swimming. Swimming! On my own, too, as Motsqueh had released his arms to let me torpedo through the water. I shot forward a good twelve feet before needing to stand, but I had done it! Motsqueh bounded forward with a loud whooping cry and jubilantly wrapped his arms around me. Startled, I returned the gesture, though I swiftly became highly cognizant of the fact we both had no clothing on whatsoever.

We continued to swim for an hour or so. I faltered, yes, more than once or twice, but I quickly learned we were not so deep as I could not stand to remedy any unsteadiness in my technique or nerves. And Motsqueh would not allow me to venture too deeply into the pond, not just yet. And I must say bathing of this stripe was far more refreshing than the baths I took at Cayuse Jem's house, as here I was wholly immersed in the placidity of the liquid itself. I found the entirety of the moment ironic. I had never considered swimming to be a pastime worthy of my endeavors; now, having learned to do it, I wished it might never end.

After an hour, or perhaps two, we tired, and we pulled ourselves out of the water and onto the grassy bank. The warm sun dried us quickly, but neither Motsqueh nor I hurried to dress again. Indeed, I was surprised by my lack of self-consciousness. I was also surprised, I must confess, by the sight of my own body. I had always been lean to the point of skinny, and pale as Banquo's ghost, as one of my old professors might say. But my form had changed while working with Cayuse Jem. I was still lean, but there was now some strength in my form and limbs. I looked older, perhaps, or perhaps this is simply what a rustic youth resembles. I must confess, comparing myself to Motsqueh, we could have been nearly twins in size and stature; even the dark hair that crowned our heads and burst forth from our pubis regions seemed to match. It was only the colors of our skin that differed.

As we lay on the grass, Motsqueh took my hand and pointed to various objects, giving me the word in his language for it and waiting for me to respond in kind. I have always been fair at languages, but Greek and Latin seem to roll off the tongue more easily than the native speech of the Nez Perce. Still, I soon learned "hísemtuks" for sun, "kús" for pond or water, "payópayo" for bird, "ácix" for turtle, "háma" for man. Motsqueh was not as quick a student, and his inability to pronounce any sounds in English longer than a single syllable proved truly droll; hearing him endeavor to say "bumblebee" had us both in giggles for several minutes.

After a time, we stopped talking, though we continued to lie on the grass, and Motsqueh continued to hold my hand. There was silence between us, but it was not uncomfortable at all. In that moment, I could not imagine reposing like this with Feldspar or Hardwicke or any other fellow I have ever known in my life. Indeed, before this afternoon, I would likely have not been able to imagine myself doing this at all. And yet, as we lay there, supine and seeming without a care in the world, it suddenly occurred to me: I have made a friend. A true and honest friend.

And then I realized, with sudden clarity: I have never had a friend before.

I turned to smile at Motsqueh, and he smiled back at me. I think—just perhaps—he felt the same.

5 August 1888

CAYUSE JEM IS proving a steady pupil; already he can read short sentences from Mr. Webster's book. He is also an excellent teacher. I am becoming quite comfortable on the horse, though after an hour or so I find my own haunches to be rather sore. I have developed a most sincere sympathy for those ranch hands who spend their days mounted on these animals. I have oft heard comic yarns in regards to the manner in which horsemen walk; having experienced precious little time in the saddle now myself, I say it is a wonder they can walk at all.

6 August 1888

I WOULD NOT suggest my equestrian skills have yet risen to the level of general competency, but I am improving every day, and Cayuse Jem tells me this is what truly matters. I have been working most frequently with a gentle mare, a sweet creature whose disposition toward me seems almost maternal at times—somehow caring and bossy all at once. Cayuse Jem laughed when I told him this. "Aye, she is the mother of this herd, that is for sure. I got her some five, six years back, off a farmer. She weren't too happy pulling a plow, but she loves looking after all the other horses, nagging at them and keeping sure they all mind their marks. Good brood mare, too. Got a talent for producing colts."

"Is that why you kept her?"

"That, and she don't have the look for a show horse. She hardly resembles an Appaloosa, though I'll be damned if her foals don't all look like leopards." It was true the horse had a particularly white coat, especially on one side, where she appeared almost wholly monochromatic.

"I don't know," I said, patting the gentle mare on the side of her nose. "I think she's quite beautiful, to be honest."

"There it is."

There was something odd about the way Cayuse Jem said those words. He spoke as if he had been expecting me to say them for some time now. "There what is, sir?"

"That look in your eye. The way you look at that mare. You can tell a lot about a man by the way he looks at a horse, I say."

I sniffed. "I do not know what you mean," I said. The mare nuzzled me on my cheek. "What is her name?"

"She ain't got a name," Cayuse Jem said.

"No? Why?"

"I don't give any of them names. Leave that to the owner. Only horse with a name is Palouse, since I'm his owner."

"But you own this horse, don't you, sir?"

"Me?" Cayuse Jem shook his head. "Naw, I don't own that horse. You do, boy."

"Pardon?" I said, not quite believing what I heard. "What did you say, sir?"

Cayuse Jem grinned. "You heard me, boy. Go on. Better give her a name. She's been waiting a long time for one."

I opened my mouth to object but knew it was ever foolish to argue with Cayuse Jem. And truth was, I didn't want to object.

"What do I call you?" I said softly to the horse, my horse, as I rubbed the underside of her powerful neck. "Huh? You are strong, you are beautiful, you are the mother to your herd... Boadicea. I shall call her Boadicea."

"Boo-dickuh?" The way the mare's new name rattled around in Cayuse Jem's mouth sounded as if he had swallowed a hedgehog. "What kind of name is that, boy?"

"Boadicea was the queen of the Iceni people in AD 61, a tribe of British Celts. She led her people in revolt against the Romans after they defiled her daughters. She is a folk hero amongst her people to this day."

Cayuse Jem considered the name. "That's a hardy woman, boy. Boadicea it is."

I placed my cheek against the side of the mare's muzzle. "Do you like the name Boadicea, girl?" In response, Boadicea rubbed against me and nickered softly.

I took that as a yes.

7 August 1888

THE PAST TWO days have been fraught with peril the likes of which I have never experienced—or ever thought I should experience—in the entirety of my eighteen years. If I have habitually complained during the penning of these passages of the tedium of rustic life, then I hope this entry will stand as stark reminder of the peaceful splendor of those dull days on the ranch I have oft protested in the past.

Our adventure began two days back, with the arrival of Chuslum and Motsqueh on our doorstep during the evening meal. I was happy to see my newfound friend, but the dark expressions on their faces clearly indicated this was not a social call. Cayuse Jem and Chuslum quickly fell into a muttered conversation at the table while I poured cups of coffee for everyone. Motsqueh paced the floor, ignoring his coffee and clearly upset, though over what I could not say.

The two men spoke in the language of the Nez Perce, but I noted Cayuse Jem and Chuslum were studying a crude, hand-drawn map of the area. I deduced the two men were discussing a place for the new Indian encampment. I held my breath. Had the situation previously discussed in this room finally come to a head?

After a terse conversation, there was a brief lull, and I dared to ask Cayuse Jem what was the matter. He hesitated before replying, but finally took me into his confidences.

"The sheriff and your father's men came to the Indian village tonight with guns. They forced the Indians to flee."

It was as I feared. "Where are they now, sir?"

"Nearby," Cayuse Jem replied. "Hiding in the woods."

I had an idea. "Can they come in here, sir? At least to the barn?"

Cayuse Jem shook his head. "Too risky. They are still on your father's land." He gave me a discerning look before continuing. "Your father's men came at sunset. In force. Told them to take what they could carry and go. The Indians watched as the men burned everything else."

I was heartily ill at the thought of these actions, all perpetrated at the command of my father. "Can they not go to the government land west of here?"

Cayuse Jem shook his head. "That's what I thought. But that land was recently sold."

"To my father?"

Cayuse Jem shook his head again. "No. To someone else." He turned to Chuslum and asked a question in the man's native language. Chuslum provided the answer. "Abernathy."

Cayuse Jem turned to me. "Do you know that name, boy?"

I nodded solemnly. "I am afraid so, sir. That man is my father's lieutenant. He is neither a kind man, nor a sympathetic one." I thought momentarily of my poor sister, slated to be married to the man. "He will not help you." I thought for another moment. "I could try speaking to my father, sir."

The tone of my voice belied my conviction that this idea would not work, and that my father would not listen to a word I would have to say on the subject matter. Nonetheless, I was willing to try.

Cayuse Jem shook his head. I suspected he knew the outcome of such a conversation as well as I. "You need to keep out of this, boy." With a loud wallop, Cayuse Jem slammed his fist on the table. I felt a pang in my stomach at this. I wanted to comfort him. I wanted to help.

"Couldn't they go to the reservation, sir, up north, near Lewiston?"

Cayuse Jem sighed, running his hand through his thick beard. "It may come to that, boy. And yet... There's little game on the land, and it's not fit for farming. The Indians who are already there... They are starving. Sickness is everywhere..."

I frowned. I worried what might happen to the Indians, to the settlers on my father's land...even to my father's men, truly. "Will the Indians fight, sir?" I asked quietly, hating to give voice to one of my greatest fears, but feeling I might burst if I did not.

Cayuse Jem pondered the question before answering. "Chuslum fought in the last war, boy. That was a bloody business, to be sure." I knew Cayuse Jem was talking about the War of 1877. I had read about the conflict—in the end, the Nez Perce forces were slaughtered, and their people were rounded up. Chuslum must have been about twenty years of age when the conflict occurred. Cayuse Jem was still speaking. "He doesn't talk about those times, but I know his people see him as a great warrior." I felt little doubt Chuslum would be a redoubtable opponent in any conflict. If he survived the war unharmed, he must have been formidable indeed.

Cayuse Jem smacked his hand hard upon the table again. "I tell you, boy, it isn't right. The government gave Chuslum's people access to all the lands around here. Then they broke their word, took it away, forced them up north, where the land isn't fit for prairie dogs." I could tell the thought of his friends being sent to the reservation distressed Cayuse Jem tremendously. I did not wish that. There must be some action I could undertake that would help.

Suddenly, I remembered something, something important. There *was* something I could do to help. Peering at the map, I pointed to a sliver of land on the eastern edge of my father's holdings. "What about here, sir?" I asked eagerly. "Could they go here?"

Cayuse Jem shook his head. "That's still your father's land, boy."

"No, sir," I said, my face beaming with excitement. "My father is not the deed holder of this land. I am."

"You?" Cayuse Jem was taken aback at this news, but already I could see his mind churning, trying to figure out how to take advantage of this new information.

"Yes, sir. My father deeded it to me for my thirteenth birthday. It was supposed to be my first foray into business. I was to attempt to develop the land for mining. But I begged to be sent to school instead, and he finally relented."

"And the land, boy?"

I shrugged my shoulders. "To my knowledge it has remained untouched this whole time, sir."

"But is it good land, boy? Good for farming, good with game? Or is it hard land, better for the mines?"

At this I had to shake my head. My cheeks flushed. "I—I do not know, sir. I never went to see it for myself. I—I wasn't interested in the land. Only in my books."

Cayuse Jem stroked his beard, deep in thought. "But it belongs to you, right, boy? Legally?"

I nodded eagerly. "Oh, yes, sir. I have the deed and everything. It is in a book in my room in the manor house." I had another thought. "If it would help, sir, I will give the land to Chuslum and his people. Outright. If it belongs to them, no one could remove them from it, yes?"

Cayuse Jem peered at me. "You would give them the land freely, boy?"

"Of course, sir, if it will help," I replied. I was excited by this idea, powerfully excited. It seemed the most natural solution. If the Indians owned the land, of course they would be safe.

Cayuse Jem placed his thick hand on my shoulder. "That is very generous of you, boy." As he spoke I thought I heard a catch in his voice. "Very generous. But I'm afraid it is against the law for Indians to own land outside of the reservation."

"Oh," I replied, falling into silence, saddened this portion of my idea to help Chuslum and Motsqueh was not viable. "I'm sorry, sir. I wanted to help."

"You have, boy. You have given us what we need. You may have saved them all."

All this time Chuslum had been silently waiting as we spoke, but I could tell he was growing impatient to understand the content of our conversation. Quickly Cayuse Jem filled him in, and I was heartened to see my news brought a light of new hope to his face.

There were still problems in need of surmounting. "I can ride out and meet the sheriff myself," Cayuse Jem was saying, to himself, perhaps, as much to me. "If I can convince him the Indians have cleared off your father's land, that may be adequate. I know him well enough. He doesn't want bloodshed if he can avoid it." He paused to stare at the map once more. "That sliver of land you own abuts this property—here. Do you know who owns that?" he asked me.

I nodded. "Yes, sir. That land belongs to Old Man Peterson—or so we always called him in our house. An irritable sort, to say the least."

"Is he a friend of your father's? An ally?"

I shook my head. "No, sir. Quite the opposite, as a matter of fact. They despise each other."

"Good. With luck, he will keep out of this fray, which will aid our cause." Cayuse Jem rose from the table and started to scramble in preparation. "It would help if we had the deed in hand," he said, "but that doesn't seem possible. Still, I think the sheriff will take my word on it, if I give it to him. And if he imagines the land belongs to this Peterson fellow, all the better. Boy, saddle up two horses. Chuslum will ride ahead and scout your land. I'll ride out and try to meet your father's men."

"Shouldn't I go, sir? I am the owner of the land in question."

Cayuse Jem shook his head. "That's too dangerous, boy."

"Sir—"

"It is not up for debate, boy. I will go alone."

At the thought of this, my blood ran cold. "Sir?" I said. "Won't that be dangerous? They may—they may not take kindly to your interfering."

Cayuse Jem took my shoulders in his hands and looked me in the eye. "I'm not going to lie to you, boy. We're taking some risks here. You understand that, don't you? If your father finds out what you have done, he will be furious. And there's no guarantee this will work. But it represents the best chance for Chuslum and his people. Do you understand?"

I swallowed. "Yes, sir."

Cayuse Jem patted me on my back. "Go saddle the horses."

I made my way by moonlight to the barn. Every fiber in my being crouched on tenterhooks, and I felt a palpable sense of dread at the evening's mission. Part of me wished I had said nothing. But Motsqueh and Chuslum were our friends, and I knew we had to help them if we could.

Motsqueh joined me in the barn. Chuslum must have updated the Indian youth on what was going on, for the anxious look on his face mirrored my own. Quickly, I saddled the horses. Motsqueh did his best to assist, though he had never saddled a horse before, so I motioned for him to open the barn doors so that they would be ready for when Cayuse Jem and Chuslum were prepared to depart.

The two men arrived moments later. I was distressed to see each carried a rifle. Cayuse Jem took my shoulder in his hand and provided me with some last-minute instructions. "Boy, you stay here. Do not leave the house tonight, under any circumstances. Understand? Motsqueh will stay with you. Look after the horses. If I am not back in two days—"

"Sir—"

"Do not interrupt me, boy. If I am not back in two days, you are to ride to the manor house. Understood?" I said nothing; I did not wish to assent to any of this. "Boy, do you understand?" I nodded.

Cayuse Jem took my face in his hands. "If all goes well, we'll be home by sunup. And we'll be mighty hungry, I'm sure."

I smiled, in spite of my fears. "I'll prepare a big breakfast, sir."

Cayuse Jem's smile was tight. "I'm sure you will, boy." He held my face a moment longer. "Nat? I want to tell you, before I go—you're a good boy, you hear me? You're a right good boy."

I nodded. "Thank you, sir."

Without another word, Cayuse Jem mounted Palouse. I could see Chuslum was having a similar conversation with Motsqueh. Then the two departed, galloping the horses out of the barn and into the night.

Motsqueh and I went back to the house. I offered him more coffee, but he had never touched the cup I originally poured for him. Nor had I drunk my own. I suppose neither of us had much stomach for it.

I cleaned up the dishes and wiped down the table. We both wanted for something to do: if not some way to help, then some task that would distract us from our worries. But there was precious little. I had my books, but even Mrs. Beeton proved an inadequate distraction.

Eventually we thought it best to try to gain some sleep, though I am unsure either of us felt actual slumber was possible. I showed Motsqueh to Cayuse Jem's bed and offered it to him. He sidled into it and pressed himself against the wall as tightly as possible. I made to plump up my own bed to make it comfortable, but Motsqueh had other ideas. Taking my hand, he drew me to him, so I was forced to clamber into Cayuse Jem's bed beside him. It was a tight fit. I had to loop my arm around the Indian lad's bare waist, and rest my cheek against his warm shoulder.

I was too anxious about the fate of Cayuse Jem and Chuslum to fret over the familiarity that resulted from our sleeping configuration. Indeed, I took some comfort from Motsqueh's presence, and I believe he must have from me, for soon the rhythmic rise and fall of his chest indicated he had drifted into sleep, fitful as it must be. I possessed no similar luck. My mind raced, and my eyes refused to close. I held Motsqueh even tighter.

It was good not to be alone.

Most evenings I fell asleep the moment my head hit my straw pillow. This night I lay awake, alert and aware to every sound the still darkness produced. I could hear the wind rustling the branches of the trees, the sound of small mammals skittering across the roof of the house, and in the distance, the baying of wolves. I missed the familiar and comforting bulk and snores of Cayuse Jem.

I hoped he would be home soon.

I must have drifted off, because I woke some time later to two distinct sounds: the panicked whinnying of the horses, and another, more distinct sound I could not quite make out—some type of angry sound, a roar, a snarl, a growl. With a sudden motion, I sat up in the bed and tried to remember if, in our grave worry over the fate of Cayuse Jem and Chuslum, I had remembered to close and seal the barn doors.

I could not remember if I had.

I sprang from the bed in an instant. I had no time to throw on my shoes. I grabbed a lantern, lit it as quickly as possible, and ran out of the house. The barn door was, indeed, open. And I could tell there was something inside.

It was a bear.

A grown horse is easily a match for a solitary coyote or wolf; a kick from their hooves, especially when shod, would send the other animal running. And we had no young foals in the barn at present. But a bear... The horses were whinnying and thrashing over this unfamiliar presence in their midst. But they clearly scented danger. Penned in their stalls, none of the horses were a match for a hungry bear.

I raced into the barn. I was unsure of what to do, but the lantern and my presence disquieted the large creature; for the present, at least, it had something new to consider. It turned toward me, and I thought, for a wild moment, if I were to draw the creature away, I might be able to lure it out of the barn and seal the doors behind it. I had a plan.

But the bear proved uncooperative. I distracted it only for a mere moment, before it turned back toward the horses, who whinnied and neighed unrelentingly. I acted swiftly. I grabbed the familiar shovel and tapped the bear on its hindquarters. I would make it pay attention to me. It worked. The bear hesitated in its advance. I struck the bear on its hindquarters again, this time harder. It turned toward me and then, in a terrifying pose, reared up on its hind legs, swatting a great forepaw at me. It missed by a hairsbreadth. I surely had the bear's attention. What do I do with it?

Out of the corner of my eye I saw Motsqueh. Somehow he had secreted behind both myself and the bear and now stood between the creature and the horses. He had several rocks in his hands and threw one, striking the bear a blow on the side of its head. The angry bear bellowed and turned toward Motsqueh. At this, he began to act strangely, waving his hands above his head and making a great deal of noise, whooping and shouting, while jumping up and down and dancing around on his feet. This strange behavior had impact, though; the bear quieted and seemed almost unnerved by the Indian youth's actions. Still clutching the shovel, I made my way toward Motsqueh and joined his movements. The bear backed up a few paces and then retreated a few more. The whinnying and neighing of the horses only added to the din, and Motsqueh and I redoubled our efforts. Finally, the bear crossed the threshold out of the barn, and we rushed to close the doors.

For a moment, we felt a sharp spasm of relief, pressing our bodies against the barn doors and inhaling great gulps of air. But now that the bear was out of visual contact with our gyrations, and now that our excessive noise had abated, the large creature became suddenly emboldened. We could only latch the doors from the inside, but not lock or seal them—the lock was on the outside. Thus, when the bear pushed against the doors, we were surprised by how far they concaved before falling back into place. The bear heaved again, and we flung our bodies against the doors in a desperate effort to keep them closed.

A third time the bear crashed against the doors, and for the third time, we barely kept them sealed. The bear was bellowing raucously, seeming enraged to have been blocked in its efforts for a significant meal. Then we could hear the bear slashing against the doors with its mighty claws. Finding this effort more futile, the bear began to explore the doors, shoving first its nose, and then a great paw, underneath the door. The first time we saw the bear's claw we jumped back instinctually, and I took the shovel and walloped the bear's hand with the flat surface of the implement. The bear withdrew its hand momentarily, but it soon reappeared. This time, I brought the sharp end of the iron spade down against the hand of the great beast. Blood spurted from the wound, and with a whelp, the animal withdrew its claw.

We heard the bear retreat a few paces, and then, silence. We waited, almost daring not to breathe. The threat of immediate danger having ceased, the horses quieted. I did a quick examination to ensure that none of them were physically wounded, and was relieved to see they were all unharmed. Panting, exhausted, I felt myself crumple to the barn floor, my back and body still pressed against the barn doors. Motsqueh joined me.

He turned to me, still catching his breath, and between pants uttered something in his own tongue. I could not understand the words, but his meaning was clear enough. "You can say that again," I replied as we leaned against the doors, and each other, for support.

8 August 1888

READING OVER THE previous entry in this journal has demonstrated to me that I did not completely finish the yarn I began yesterday. It is perhaps because, second to experiencing the actual events themselves, recording them proved almost as exhausting. Though I suppose the mere fact I am still here to make entries in my journal should indicate that Motsqueh and I made it through our little adventure relatively unscathed, even after I told Cayuse Jem all about it.

We must have drifted off perched against the door, for we woke with Cayuse Jem and Chuslum staring at us and rousing us to wakefulness. Cayuse Jem looked around, noting with his keen eyes my bare feet, the claw marks on the door, and the blood stains on the ground. "You two seem to have had an adventure," he said, giving me a hand to lift me from the dirt floor of the barn while checking me over for injuries most assiduously.

Chuslum was doing the same for Motsqueh and speaking to him in their own tongue in rapid-fire bursts. Then the two embraced quite sincerely, and Chuslum covered Motsqueh's face in kisses. I admit myself embarrassed by this behavior and turned away, though I supposed it merely a custom of their tribe and also a presaging of the success of the two men's endeavors. I confess I also found Chuslum's actions endearingly affectionate and found myself, red-cheeked, turning back to witness the culmination of the exchange.

But there were more pressing matters at hand. In response to my query about his success, Cayuse Jem gave such a great smile that it could not even be concealed by his shaggy beard or the weary lines of his face. "Chuslum guided his people to their new land, and I convinced the sheriff the Indians had left your father's property. Indeed, the sheriff was so ready for a warm meal and his bed that it did not take much convincing at all."

"And the land, sir?" I asked. "Is it suitable for the purpose?"

Cayuse Jem nodded his assent. "Chuslum tells me it is rich in game. It will take some work to clear the land for planting, but the soil is good. And there is a small stream that runs through to provide them with water." He paused before speaking again. "I daresay, boy, if it was your father's intent for you to mine the land, well, I don't think you'd have made much of a go of it. It's not mining land at all. But for Chuslum's people..." Cayuse Jem broke off, but no more needed to be said. As for me, I was glad my father's lack of largesse worked so adroitly against him.

At this moment, Chuslum came up to me. Taking my shoulders in his hands, he spoke to me in his own tongue, and though I did not comprehend what he was saying, I did understand that he was conveying his gratitude. I did my best to shrug off his appreciation—in the end, I had contributed very little—but Chuslum crushed me in his arms in a great bear hug. I was engulfed in the totality of the large man, his broad chest and strong arms covering the entirety of my face, and was embarrassed to be on the receiving end of such an affectionate response. Embarrassed, but not altogether unpleased. Motsqueh, too, understanding that his people had a new home, bounded over to me with arms wide open, covering my cheek with small kisses and laughing happily. The last recognition came from the arms of Cayuse Jem himself, who held me close even when I moved to pull away.

"You are the hero, boy," he said into my ear. "You saved the day."

I blushed at his words. "I did nothing, sir, truthfully."

Cayuse Jem smiled and continued to hold me in his arms. To be honest, I did not mind him holding me. Not one whit. "Now, boy," he said, "do you care to explain why we found you asleep in the barn?"

And thus I was compelled to tell Cayuse Jem all about the incident with the bear. Motsqueh did his best to aid my story, and his impersonation of the bear might have been comical had it not brought back several shivering memories. Our adventure earned us a stern talking-to from Cayuse Jem in both English and Nez Perce—truly, the first time I have been admonished in dual languages—and a sharp swat on the rear for having left the barn door open. It was certainly less than I deserved, and explanations done, we bade goodbye to Chuslum and Motsqueh and went about our day.

After such grand adventures, one would think we had earned some rest. Though I had slept the previous night, it was but a scant few hours, and Cayuse Jem had not slept at all. Still, there were animals to tend to and chores to be completed, and thus we fell back into our daily schedule. I confess I did not mind so much. After so much intrigue, routine felt—well, blessedly routine.

9 August 1888

BY HAPPENSTANCE, WE received two visitors today at the ranch: Mr. Mackey, the peddler-man, and my father.

Both calls were unanticipated, though I suppose circumstances should have prefigured their visits. Mr. Mackey arrived first, and he brought with him twenty-one new tomes for my now burgeoning collection. Several of the books were rather tattered and worn; clearly, Mr. Mackey had purchased most of these from other customers on his route. I did not care. I took eager possession of all of them, much to Cayuse Jem's amusement.

The peddler-man had amassed a somewhat unique trove of texts. There were multiple women's novels, a few more texts by Mr. Alger, and some from Mr. Fenimore Cooper; an almanac, a pharmacopoeia, and a more extensive lexicon by Mr. Webster; several collections of religious verse; and a few works of literary value—a book of Mr. Pope's essays, two works by Jane Austen, *Uncle Tom's Cabin*, and a battered copy of Mr. Dickens' *Bleak House*.

Though I was excited by such a wide array of texts, it was the pharmacopoeia that most intrigued me. The events of the last few days have weighed heavily on my mind. Mrs. Beeton had taught me much about cooking, and I had used the knowledge I gleaned from her book in helpful, practical ways. I wondered if I might apply the same philosophy to the pharmacopoeia. I suspected, in this life, it would be advantageous to have some knowledge of medicine and herbal lore—and the pharmacopoeia contained all of the latest medical knowledge available. I knew, at the very least, it certainly could not hurt. I only hoped it would never truly be necessary.

My father's visit was even more unexpected. I had gone to the stream to draw water and returned just in time to see my father climbing into his brougham. I hurried in order to meet him, but even though I saw him glance in my direction, he did not linger, but rather continued on his way with nary a pause.

I continued to hurry, dropping the water as I half ran, half scampered my way to where my father's brougham had been. Yet by the time I arrived, I could only spy the cloud of dust left behind in my father's wake.

"What did he say?" I finally asked Cayuse Jem, when I was capable of speaking again.

"We talked about the horses, mostly."

"Did he say anything about me?"

"He said he wants you back by middle of October, for your sister's wedding."

"Did he say anything else?" I peered at Cayuse Jem. "Did he ask about me—at all?" Somberly, Cayuse Jem shook his head.

Without another word, I went back to fetch the pails of water I had dropped.

That evening, as I worked with Cayuse Jem on his reading, I felt the large man beside me very gently, and very consolingly, place his arm around my shoulder. For my part, I bent my head into the ample crook made by the union of Cayuse Jem's arm and shoulder and wept.

10 August 1888

I ONCE WEPT in front of my father. I was nine, and my dog Falstaff had just been killed in front of me, run over by the wheels of a carriage that was pulling into the manor house.

My father, seeing the dead dog and my contorted face, struck me hard, twice, violently forcing me into silence. It was—at least in his mind, I would wager—my first true lesson in manhood.

Last night, Cayuse Jem did no such thing as I wept into his arm. Instead, he let me weep, held me, and when my lament began to abate, he kissed me on my forehead twice and sent me to sleep in his bed.

I do not know what kind of man I am, or what kind of man I shall become. I do know, however, what kind of man I admire.

11 August 1888

WHEN I BEGAN once again to write in this journal I posited, in my own inestimably naïve way, that I should be writing only about those times in my life I will not wish to remember, that my experiences back in the territory would only include those occurrences I should wish to forget, or that would never be worth memorializing.

I am happy, once more, to have been unequivocally wrong in my assumptions.

Last night, after I bathed Cayuse Jem's broad shoulders and backside, he leaned back solidly against the metal of the tub. "Boy," he said, "will you bathe my front too?" I agreed with nary a word nor thought. Feeling the brush too rough for this more delicate portion of the man's body, I soaped my hands as lavishly as I could and began to rub them vigorously through the thick hair of Cayuse Jem's chest. Round and round I went, creating whorls of soap and water as the thick coat of his russet-colored hair mesmerized me. His flesh felt soft and hard all at once, a perfect emblem, really, of Cayuse Jem himself. My hands steadily moved lower, over the firm round belly and to the sides of his haunches. It was then, I saw, through the soap in the water, Cayuse Jem's loins, and his member, now engorged to the point of straining. "Boy," Cayuse Jem quite simply said. "Don't you think it is time."

It was not a question, not really, but rather a statement. It made me think of a bit of gossip I heard somewhat frequently whilst I was still at Harvard. It was rumored amongst the boys that Professor Richman, who taught Greek language and literature, had initiated a small group of students into his private inner circle. There he shared with them forbidden texts that talked about the nature and act of the sin of the Greeks, the "love that dare not speak its name," as the rather stodgy head of the Greek department, Dr. Browne, referred to it on more than one occasion. I frequently imagined Professor Richman in his study, surrounded by three or four eager youths who listened to him as he read and lectured, taking great comfort and solace in the words that trickled forth from the pages before them. I imagined what it meant to them to know that someone, somewhere, even two thousand years ago, had felt the same as they, felt the same longings and felt the same furtive desires. His words must have been a balm for their souls. This was a secret history to which I would never be privy, which I would never know.

I took a class with Professor Richman, in my second semester at university. I wanted him to select me for his coterie, to pluck me out of the crowd and understand some part of me I could neither articulate nor hope to understand myself. I wanted him to do this without even understanding what it meant or even without knowing I wanted it at all. I wanted this thing, wanted it more than I had ever wanted anything before, all without truly knowing I wanted or needed it. It is perhaps ironic that, at the beginning of this journal, I pondered whether I even had such desires.

No wonder I was so bewildered.

Professor Richman did not notice me, or if he did, he never gave recognition to such notice. Perhaps there was some special knowledge, some secret code I did not possess in order to gain entry to that world. But, then again, it was not even a world into which I knew I wished entry. My hopes and desires were simply an instinct then, and nothing more.

All of this ran through my mind as Cayuse Jem lay before me, his member engorged, his innermost desire apparent for all to see. "Boy?" Some scant moments had passed since his earlier statement, and lost in my reverie, I had neglected to answer him promptly.

I would not make that error again.

"Yes, sir," I simply said. And I smiled. And I stood, removed my own garments, and stepped into the warm soapy water with Cayuse Jem, resting my back against his broad chest.

He wrapped his large arms around my waist, and I rested my head against him. He took the soap and rubbed my body with it—my chest, my stomach, my own engorged member and loins. "You do understand what is happening, boy, yes?"

"Yes, sir," I sighed.

"And how do you feel about it?"

I half twisted, half contorted my body so that my cheek was pressed against the wooly hair of Cayuse Jem's body. The sensation of that thick mat of hair against the soft blush of my cheek—I lack the language to describe such a phenomenon. With the studied air of a scientist and the fervent zeal of a lad on Christmas morning I plunged my hands under the water to clutch at Cayuse Jem's engorged member. Like the rest of him, it had features of hard and soft, rigid in its turgid construction and yet fleshy and warm, much like the rest of the man.

"I am most happy, sir," I said.

In response, Cayuse Jem kissed me.

I imagine my sister has frequently envisaged what her first kiss will be like. She is a woman, after all, and I am led to believe women oft ponder such things. And she is soon to be wed, to that odious Abernathy, so perhaps it is foremost in her mind. But I had never before pondered this moment, so the absolute joy of it caught me wholly unawares. And most contentedly so.

Cayuse Jem took my chin in his hand, positioned my mouth, and moved his lips slowly toward me. By some instinct, I extended my own lips to meet his. I had imagined I would feel the bristle and hackle of his beard when we kissed, and it was there, but only in the background. Rather I felt the intense warmth inherent in the extended, fleshy lips of the man and there, beyond the warmth, another kind of heat, one sharp as filed steel. I was caught unawares and, momentarily, ceased to breathe.

This, I later came to know, was desire.

I collapsed against his chest, the weight of this occasion dazzling the very innermost parts of my body and soul. If I was a horse, Cayuse Jem might suggest that, perhaps, I had been bred for a moment like this. But as I am a far different kind of creature, I could do naught but return Cayuse Jem's kiss with as much emotion and devotion as I could muster.

We dawdled some time in that metal tub, kissing, my lean form crumpled against the thick hewn meat of Cayuse Jem. Cayuse Jem kissed me sweetly, kissed me fiercely, kissed me as I understand the French kiss, with his tongue inserted into my mouth. How I longed for more. And the hair on his chest held endless fascination for me, and his beard—that thick, russet beard!—when he kissed my ear or neck how it tickled, how it made my heart skip with pleasure. My hands did their best to explore the immense masculinity of Cayuse Jem, but they seemed ever drawn to his loins, to his engorged member, that fleshy continuation of his greater self and being. When I squeezed it just so,

Cayuse Jem half closed his eyes, and a small sound of contentment would escape from his lips. I was pleasing him, and it pleased me to recognize this.

For his part, Cayuse Jem oft rested his hands on my buttocks. At first I thought this merely a convenient place to lay his hands—we were quite enclosed in the tub—but then I realized his motions held greater purpose. His fingers massaged my haunches, and spread each cheek apart delicately, finding a part of me I was unsure even existed. There—back there—Cayuse Jem sought what he must have always known was present and rested one of his thick digits against the secret entrance place to a world I would soon know much more about. Then—with a rather startled but exultant gasp on my part—Cayuse Jem slipped his finger inside of me.

I felt—I felt—it is difficult to put into words what I felt. I felt as if we were at the beginning of some extraordinary process, a process determined to make us two into one person, one soul. I thought of Plato in *The Symposium* and the splitting of the soul into two. When one half of the soul finds its mate, the two become as one, and that is how I felt at that moment with Cayuse Jem. That may sound like a rather grandiose claim, but in my experience, and judging by what happened afterward, it is rather more a statement of plain fact than anything else.

I am unsure how long we stayed like this, our lips entwined, my body prone against the manly form of Cayuse Jem, his fingers moving in and out of my nether-eye with the dexterity of a musician playing his favorite instrument. As player and apparatus we made our own music, Cayuse Jem's small grunts and minor roars supplemented, and often overcome, by the contented sighs and moans emanating from my own throat. I am sure I would have been pleased to stay like that all night, but the water began to cool and, eventually, grew cold, and Cayuse Jem released his digits from my nether region and ordered me out of the tub.

I complied.

I fetched the towel and dried him off. His member...now that I could truly see it, the immensity and weight of it... This is how an apostate must feel upon finding proof of God. I longed to please it, that much I knew, but as to how... I had little concern in my heart. Cayuse Jem would teach me.

He had taught me so much already.

Once dry, Cayuse Jem lifted me in his arms and carried me to his bed. I thought he might fling me down, as in a Gothic novel, but instead, ever-so-gently, he placed me on his sheets. I imagined he might lay on top of me and the rutting would commence, but instead, Cayuse Jem planted his feet near the head of the bed.

"I'm going to teach you how to please me now, boy," he said. His voice was gentle, and his hand reached out to stroke my cheek. I eagerly grabbed it with my own. His hand was so large, so strong, so substantial. "Is that something you would like to learn?"

"Oh, yes, sir," I contentedly replied.

Cayuse Jem used his index finger to trace the soft curve of my face. He pressed the digit against my lips, and I instinctually opened my mouth. Cayuse Jem inserted his finger past my lips, and I suckled it eagerly, like a lamb suckling his mother's teat. Removing his one finger, he slipped two in its stead, and I suckled ever more eagerly, to demonstrate my dedication to Cayuse Jem's pleasure. I was amazed I did all of this without an act of conscious thought; it seemed innate to me, something born deep inside. Cayuse Jem slipped his fingers out of my mouth. "You're ready, boy," he whispered huskily before placing the thick apex of his engorged member near my lips. Though it was much wider than his finger, I did my best to suckle it in my mouth, taking, at first, only the tip, and then determining to take in as much as I could.

I'm afraid my technique was far from perfect; "Watch your teeth, boy," Cayuse Jem said more than once, and I did my best to ensure that only my soft lips touched his most private part. I kissed his flesh; caressed it with my tongue and cheek and hand; ran my tongue up and down the thick, veined shaft of his member, all as Cayuse Jem instructed. Per his directions, I slid my tongue between the tight enfold of his glans and his hood; swirling my tongue around, I felt a salty, warm sensation permeate my mouth, a dribbling of liquid that caused me momentary alarm. But a chuckling Cayuse Jem assured me such events were normal in the course of what we were doing, and I should eagerly take in as much of the liquid he produced as I could.

I heartily obeyed.

I would learn to do this better; like cooking, I hoped that, with practice and study, my art would improve. This was important to me, and I wished to convey my outlook to Cayuse Jem. But for the moment, he had placed his large, hirsute testicles over my face, and I was instructed to "bathe them with your tongue, boy."

At one point, Cayuse Jem leaned over and inhaled my own engorged member into his mouth. I was nowhere near as large as Cayuse Jem, but I was rigidly upright, almost painfully so. But the pleasure that coursed through me when Cayuse Jem placed all of me in his mouth was unlike anything I had ever felt. I gasped so loudly and so effusively that Cayuse Jem's testicles slipped from my face, only to be replaced once more by the thick shaft of his own engorged member. I began to kiss and lick this part of him again, and

Cayuse Jem's joyful moaning sounds indicated my actions were pleasing to him. My own member tingled with new sensations; Cayuse Jem's mouth was like a warm, inviting cavern, damp and dark, and I felt as if I were an explorer discovering a new world. His beard tickled my stomach, and I craned my neck in order to please as much of Cayuse Jem as I could.

I felt a sudden and unexpected heightening of sensation in my loins. The feeling came upon me with such speed and alacrity I was barely able to extricate Cayuse Jem's member from my mouth and call out a simple warning of "Sir!" before streams of warm, white liquid escaped from my member and splashed Cayuse Jem all over his face and beard. I thought he would be displeased over this, or disconcerted, but Cayuse Jem's response was a big, hearty laugh. "I think that means you like me, boy," he said, using the towel to wipe his face.

"I love you, sir," I bravely replied.

I had never said those words, not in all of my life. Not to Father, nor to Grandmomma, nor even to Dora. I had read them, read of the emotion of love, but had never really considered it seriously until now, until this very moment. But then I realized this is what love is: not the physical acts we were committing, but the devotion I felt, the desire to please, the desire for union with Cayuse Jem. This was love, at least in how I knew I should always experience it.

Cayuse Jem climbed into the bed with me and lay on top of me. He held me gently in his arms. His belly pushed into me, but the weight of him on top of me was a pleasant phenomenon; I felt protected and secure with Cayuse Jem on top of me, more safe than I had ever felt before, more safe and secure in this world than I even perceived was possible. "Boy," he said thickly. "I love you, boy, more than anyone I have ever known, more than anyone I ever will. Do you believe me when I tell you that, boy?"

I wrapped my arms around Cayuse Jem's thick neck. "Yes, sir."

Cayuse Jem placed his hand to his mouth and spit into his palm—once, then twice. He reached down and rubbed the spit onto his engorged member. He used his broad hips to push my legs apart. "This is how I show love, boy," he whispered in my ear. I felt the head of his member pushing against the recess of my backside. "This is how I show love." With one of his arms he crooked my right leg up, bending it perpendicular to the bed. Now that I was fully exposed, Cayuse Jem pushed the head of his engorged member deep inside of me.

I had long been cognizant of the sin of the Greeks; I knew, in all practical theory, what was being referred to when I heard those words being uttered. But I had never truly conceived what that sin might convey, or how those actions might look or feel. Now, here, with Cayuse Jem, I was struck first by the fullness of it all. As Cayuse Jem penetrated me, as he moved deeper inside of me, as I watched his face transfigure into an ecstatic expression, almost saint-like in its devotional aspect, and as I felt myself being subsumed by Cayuse Jem and his engorged member, I experienced an incredible sense of wholeness; that my own self was somehow being made complete, and that Cayuse Jem was filling not only my backside and my nether region but those blank spaces I had not known existed in my own heart and soul. Tears sprang from my eyes, and Cayuse Jem assumed them to be tears of pain and halted in his movements, and whispered sweet words of consolation in my ear. I shook my head, but I was too transfixed by the moment, by the curious sensation of feeling complete for the first time in my life, by happiness and yes, absolutely, too transfixed by love, to speak any words to the contrary to this man who had made me whole, and happy, and who gave me such tremendous love in his turn. I understood everything in that moment, and in my desire to show my understanding to Cayuse Jem, I reached down, grabbed his haunches, and thrust him even deeper inside me, bringing the moment closer to fruition, merging our two souls and beings ever more into one.

Cayuse Jem understood; he began to move back and forth inside me in a steady, measured rhythm. I squeezed Cayuse Jem's neck and bore down. There was some pain in this, yes, but it did not hurt me at all. Indeed, it gave me great pleasure, and an even greater pleasure to know I was pleasing Cayuse Jem, satisfying him, and that our union brought tremendous joy to both of us. How could anyone ever label this action the sin of the Greeks? This was no sin; a more holy union I could not imagine.

Cayuse Jem locked his lips onto mine; his beard prickled my chin and my nipples, and my body sang with sensation. He thrust faster inside me, deeper, until a joyous barking sound began to emanate from his lips. I felt that same sensation from before in my own loins at almost precisely the same moment; as I felt my innards being flooded with Cayuse Jem's seed, my own member spilled again, and Cayuse Jem's belly was coated with the product of our congress.

There was little speech afterward; there was no need for it. Twice more that night Cayuse Jem lay with me, penetrating my regions with his self. Twice more I experienced the purest happiness I believe I am capable of knowing. And afterward, without fail, Cayuse Jem held me, and as he held me, that silent, taciturn man whispered such things in my ear as to make me blush: heartfelt expressions of love and desire the likes of which I have not ever read in a book.

As I read over the words I have penned in this entry, I wonder if it is prudent to put such practice to paper. Well, this journal is for me. It is a record of remembrance.

And I shall not wish to forget this night for as long as I shall live upon this earth.

15 August 1888

SINCE SETTLING ON their new land, Chuslum and Motsqueh have been regular visitors to our home. I always looked forward to these visits, especially from the youth whom I already considered to be my closest companion in the world—saving, of course, for Cayuse Jem, who was closer to me than any man, any individual, or any being could or would ever be. And yet these past few days have been marked by their absence, which I confess I had not noticed, distracted as I have been by the newfound love that is growing between myself and Cayuse Jem and my continuing lessons in the art of pleasing a man.

I believe I have learned quite a bit about this latest area of study. I have learned, for example, that Cayuse Jem grows ever more invigorated when performing his—duties—if I create ample noise, and even more vitalized if I plead to him as he is thrusting into me. I have learned that rotating my tongue underneath the skin found on the head of his glans is always sure to elicit both a happy moan and a pearlescent drop of a white substance of whose name I am yet unsure, but whose flavor becomes ever more familiar to me with each passing day. I have learned, too, that there are ample delights in merely being held by Cayuse Jem, by lying in the crook of his bare arm and falling asleep with the hairs found in the region underneath his arm's notch tickling my nose, the musky aroma of the man filling my every breath and dream. Oh yes, I have learned much in these past few days about this new art of pleasing, though I also realize I have much still to learn.

It is a subject to which I have happily pledged much sincere dedication.

One thing I did not know, for example, at least not until I saw my two Indian friends making their way across the paddock and to the barn early this afternoon, is that the relationship between Chuslum and Motsqueh mirrored that of Cayuse Jem and myself. And yet it was so startlingly obvious! What a thick-headed fool I have been! Their easy manner, their understanding, their affectionate conduct, the way Chuslum tends to and cares for Motsqueh, the way Motsqueh looks to Chuslum for guidance and leadership—it was such a palpable equivalence to my own newfound relations that I chastened myself for not seeing it earlier.

Of course, there were a great many things I had not earlier seen, until Cayuse Jem opened my eyes to them.

It seemed apparent, though, that our friends understood the nature of change in the relationship between Cayuse Jem and myself; Chuslum's broad smile indicated his pleasure at this new turn of events, while Motsqueh kept repeating a phrase over and over that Cayuse Jem finally translated as a Nez Perce expression that indicated that such activities between us were long overdue. I must profess that, initially, the fact that Chuslum and Motsqueh had knowledge—indeed, rather intimate and experienced knowledge, judging from their own example—of the nocturnal activities that transpired between Cayuse Jem and myself made me blush; and yet, the more I thought on it, the more I delighted that these close companions had suddenly grown ever more intimate. We were a family now, in a way; an odd little family, to be sure, but nonetheless, I heartened at the thought of it.

Motsqueh aided me in my afternoon's chores so that we might enjoy some time together, a "boy's holiday," as Cayuse Jem referred to it. We dashed through the woods to our swimming hole and plunged in, enjoying the cool waters on our bare skin. I was certainly less hesitant to shuck my clothing in front of Motsqueh now, as my evenings with Cayuse Jem had taught me not to be embarrassed by what is both natural and pure.

After a quick romp in the waters, Motsqueh and I got down to the business at hand—talking about our beaux. I felt like a gossipy bride as we endeavored, through sign and sound, to share both our joys and frustrations at being the beloved boys to such men as Cayuse Jem and Chuslum. At the beginning of this summer I could not have imagined ever engaging in any such conversation in my life—not on the subject matter, surely, and not even with my fellow conversant. And yet, here I was, as content as I could imagine being. As we conversed, Motsqueh and I sat perched against the rough-hewn bark of a willow tree, its branches providing us shade and shield from the obdurate August sun. Motsqueh began by running his hands through my hair and then over my chest, which I took as a question about the hairy nature of Cayuse Jem's body. I nodded and laughed and growled in impersonation of the bear we had previously encountered, noting a similarity between the furry mammal and the presentation of Cayuse Jem. Motsqueh smiled broadly and added his own impersonation, and we growled in mock ferocity at one another and then laughed until our sides ached. I also assured Motsqueh, though, by cozying up to the soft grass that cushioned our forms, that I enjoyed each and every hirsute portion of Cayuse Jem immensely.

With an impish glance Motsqueh then placed his hand above his body's crutch, and particularly above his pubis region. At first I was unsure of what he was inquiring, but then I realized he was wondering how large Cayuse Jem becomes when fully engorged. I blushed but obliged, placing Motsqueh's hand approximately seven inches above his body.

Motsqueh seemed impressed. "Chuslum?" I asked, pointing at Motsqueh's hand. Instantly, the hand raised another two inches, perhaps a bit more. "You are not serious," I gasped, but this only earned me a quizzical glance from my boon friend. I took a more direct approach. "No," I said, shaking my head and smiling to indicate that I thought Motsqueh was joshing with me. But Motsqueh nodded his head in great earnestness. "Really?" And then, as if to prove it, Motsqueh stood, and then squatted, as if mounting Chuslum, and screwed up his face in such a contortion that we both ended up rolling across the grass in another fit of utter hysterics.

We finally ceased chortling, ending up supine on our backs in the cool grass. Motsqueh took my hand in his, and there we rested, our heads touching in solidarity and friendship, watching the clouds and thanking our creators for the many blessings we had been given. But all too soon, it was time to begin the preparation of the evening meal, and thus time to head home.

Chuslum and Motsqueh were invited to stay, but declined. Their absence, though, provided me an opportunity to learn more about my friends. "Motsqueh has no relations," Cayuse Jem told me, in response to my initial query. "His father died many years back, when he was but a babe, in a skirmish with some settlers. His mother died about three years ago, of sickness. Chuslum took him in, looked after him, helped him."

"Much as you have me, sir," I said to Cayuse Jem, reaching across the table to take his hand in mine. Cayuse Jem smiled, dunking the homemade bread I had made yesterday in his venison stew before taking a large bite.

"Chuslum was a great warrior in his youth," Cayuse Jem said. "But all he ever wanted for his people was peace. And he has tried his best to lead them that way." He took another bite of the bread. "When Motsqueh came of age, they were joined. The Indians understand how it sometimes is between two men. They don't condemn it; they bless it."

"Motsqueh is very lucky to be with Chuslum," I said. "Just as I am lucky to be yours, sir."

Cayuse Jem dropped the remaining hunk of bread on the table. Pulling on my arm, he drew me to his lap and wrapped his strong limbs around me. "I love you, boy," he said thickly.

"And I love you, sir," I replied. Cayuse Jem placed one of his burly hands against the back of my head and brought my lips to his. I could feel his loins heating and hastened to strip him of his garments so I might better please him.

The cobbler I had made for dessert would have to wait.

19 August 1888

I SUPPOSE I should apologize to my journal for my periodic absences from its pages. I simply seem to have no time nor inclination to spend my hours writing, when I have so much more to do.

My days are filled with toil, and with the lessons Cayuse Jem provides about the horses. In the evening, I teach Cayuse Jem to read. At night...at night, I have other lessons, as Cayuse Jem teaches me to please him and about how two men share love.

This is learning I shall never tire of, no matter how hard I work to master it.

Last night, I enjoyed a rather peculiar but transcendent experience. Several days ago, Cayuse Jem initiated me into the practice wherein he places his tongue into my own nether region, to properly prepare me for the insertion of his member. The first time I experienced this sensation... I felt as if I were suspended in midair, a bird soaring through the heavens, as if my soul had briefly been transported out of my body. I showered Cayuse Jem with my liquids right then and there, and how he delighted to see my intense enjoyment of the moment. Last night I was instructed to return the favor. I leaned against the wall of our home and Cayuse Jem stood afore me, his large haunches bent. There they were before me, suffused with russet hair and promising a dark and mysterious adventure, one that, I admit, I was a bit apprehensive about embarking upon. But

I did as instructed, and to my surprise, a world of pungent delight revealed itself to me. It was not nearly as malodorous as I feared; the scent was musky and strong, but not altogether unpleasant. Furthermore, when I buried my small face into Cayuse Jem's large haunches, I felt almost lost, as if every sense with which I am capable of experiencing sensation was filled, wholly and completely, with only Cayuse Jem. I should have known in my heart to trust Cayuse Jem utterly. Indeed, I felt so lost in the moment I was hardly aware when Cayuse Jem pulled away from me, whirled around, and slammed his member deep into my mouth and throat, filling my gullet with every drop of his manly seed.

But I was quite pleased to receive each and every morsel.

So this is what my days and nights consist of now. There is precious little time to write. I fear I shall continue to be an ill correspondent.

But I have rather more important things to do.

22 August 1888

IT OCCURS TO me that, in all this time I have known Cayuse Jem, whilst I have been curious as to the origin of his name—indeed, I even asked my father what it meant—I have never asked the source directly about its meaning. I am unsure why this is so, and what is perhaps even more puzzling, I remain reluctant to do so. Perhaps because Cayuse Jem has already shown me the answers to so many questions, questions I did not even know to ask, that I feel as I though I should perhaps answer this one on my own.

And then I remembered that Mr. Mackey had delivered to me a more comprehensive dictionary, and I thought to look in there for the answer. And sure enough, there it was. As for the word's meaning, this is what Mr. Webster has to say: "Cayuse: A small pony, especially a recalcitrant one. A Northwest colloquialism." Hmm. Discovering the definition of the term did little to help me understand the meaning of his name. After all, Cayuse Jem was hardly a pony—he was a stallion, to be sure—but perhaps the moniker was meant ironically? Though that seemed odd to me. And I do not think any just man could justly describe Cayuse Jem as recalcitrant. This is not because Cayuse Jem was, as a man, easy to handle or given to other's control—indeed, the very opposite is the truth! It is simply that, as a word, "recalcitrant" enjoins such a negative connotation. A difficult person is not a pleasant thing at all. But Cayuse Jem is not difficult in any traditional sense of the word—or, indeed, in any sense of the word at all. He is a natural-born leader. Strong. Dominant, yes. Absolutely. He possesses an inherent ability to direct and command, though I could hardly see in what capacity these qualities—in him—could be considered an undesirable trait. For someone like my father, his recalcitrance renders him...unpleasant. But for Cayuse Jem, it just makes him...well, it makes him a man.

24 August 1888

I WAS AT work today in the stables, bent over the rail of Palouse's stall, when I felt a familiar pair of hands roughly clutch my hips. "Boy," I heard, more a distinct growl than an interpretable utterance, and I could feel the now-familiar presence of Cayuse Jem's enlarged member, straining against his trousers, being rubbed against my backside.

"Sir," I said, maintaining my bent-over stance, my voice saucy with craft, "do you mean to take me here and now, in the middle of the workday, in the stables?" Whilst I was saying this, I was also rubbing my arse against the swollen protuberance that now defined the front of Cayuse Jem's trousers.

I hope it is evident that I have been learning well my lessons in how to please Cayuse Jem.

Cayuse Jem's hands roughly pushed my breeches and underclothing down to my knees, and I could feel him undo the buttons that restrained his member. I heard him spit once onto his hands and then, a mere moment later, felt the familiar, welcome sensation of the head of Cayuse Jem's member pressed against the split in my backside. A moment passed and my flesh yielded, and the first prized inches of Cayuse Jem's member pushed aggressively inside me. I gasped, as I always do when asked to accommodate the immensity and substance of the man I prized above all others. Another few moments and Cayuse Jem was now fully inside me, roughly, violently, holding me tightly in his hands for a moment before he began the to-and-fro thrusting that always accompanied our lovemaking. And, indeed, this was lovemaking, though this was not the long, slow, unhurried lovemaking we shared each evening, when blushing words of affection passed our lips, when I traced my name in the hairs of Cayuse Jem's chest, and when our slow dance of devotion could end in any of a half dozen sodden, delicious possibilities. No, this was ardor of a wholly different sort: this was about possession as much as love; this was about the assertion of one will over another; this was about the shaping of roles and the establishment of a collective, corrective hierarchy.

This is just one of the many imperative lessons I have learned since coming to this ranch and falling under the tutelage of Cayuse Jem, and I smiled with immense fulfillment as Cayuse Jem completed his amorous exertions in short order, spilling his seed deep inside me before pulling up his trousers and taking a step back, his breath still coming in short, ragged gasps, the red of his cheeks suggesting both the heat of the August midday sun and the passion he felt for me. It only remained for me to pull up my breeches; my stiff member, ignored and still turgid inside my trousers, would be tended to later tonight.

Of course, Cayuse Jem being the man he is, being the sort of man he is, and having the sort of feeling for me he does, can never leave such a moment without taking me in his arms, holding me closely, kissing my forehead and face a round half dozen times, and whispering in my ear, "You're the best boy, Nat, the best. You really are, boy." And then he peppered my face with another volley of kisses, held my cheeks in his hands, and then, with one last look, left me to go about the business of the day.

Oh, yes, I know precisely what these types of encounters mean. Curiously, I am unsure if Cayuse Jem himself is aware of their significance. Does he understand what these encounters portend, or is he merely capitulating to his more amorous desires?

It is certainly curious, to be sure, and a question upon which I will need to expend some thought before I can determine an answer.

26 August 1888

TODAY WAS SUNDAY, and Motsqueh and I were allowed another boy's holiday after the midday repast. "You shall be in danger of spoiling me at this rate," I said to Cayuse Jem with an impish grin, a response that earned me a distinctive swat on my backside—and a small smile—as we made our way out of the house.

Back we went to our favorite swimming hole. We romped and splashed for a bit, and then began to do as we always did on such occasions—gossip about the men in our lives. Though we still could not converse in any traditional sense of the term (Cayuse Jem had started to teach me small bits and pieces of the Nez Perce language, but to this point, I had only grasped the most fundamental syntax structure of the tongue and had a tremendously limited vocabulary; thus my insufficient knowledge was hardly useful for carrying on a dialogue), we could, through gesture, through expression, through pantomime, and through our own sympathetic understanding of the other, truly communicate a good deal. There was an understanding between us, one derived in part from our shared situation, but one that had also developed—as I have come to believe—from the great bond between us. I have oft read in stories and books that best friends are defined by the fact that they share a bond that allows them to know the other infinitely well, to communicate in methods of shorthand incomprehensible to the outside world. And so it seemed for Motsqueh and myself.

Of course, there were some situations I still found difficult to convey to Motsqueh, no matter how diligently I attempted to do so. I felt a great longing to ask Motsqueh about some of my more recent encounters with Cayuse Jem and what these exchanges might mean in terms of our relationship. I wondered if Chuslum altered long nights of passion and romantic love with brief bursts of intense carnality, and what Motsqueh thought of such encounters. But these were questions of a metaphysical variety that were perhaps too difficult to convey in only gestures and facial expressions.

Then again, perhaps not. At one point, as we lounged together on the grass, and as I struggled to explain my questions to Motsqueh about these varying romantic interludes with Cayuse Jem, Motsqueh placed his index finger on my forehead. Holding it there for a moment, he then swatted my skin, causing me to flinch momentarily, more in surprise than in any painful response. Then he leaned over, kissed my forehead, and turned on his back, nestling himself into the grass as if to settle in more comfortably. I did the same, though my brow was still furrowed in thought. And then I recollected that my sister Dora would perpetrate the very same action whenever I—as a small child—peppered her with so many questions that I would transform from the average, work-a-day pesky younger sibling into a fount of continual, fraternal annoyance. Her little "love taps"—as she labeled them— were her way of resetting my mind, to encourage me to focus on one item at a time. Perhaps the situation was similar here, and Motsqueh was merely trying to tell me that I am simply thinking too much about my current state of affairs. After all, every encounter with Cayuse Jem—whether protracted or concise, whether romantic or wanton—

thrilled me. Every moment being his boy was the new best moment of my life. Yes, dissecting these moments may prove a fruitful exercise for my mind and may help me to better understand my role in this new relationship. But, in the end, they mattered little in how I felt about Cayuse Jem, and how he felt for me. Love is love is love is love, and perhaps that is all I needed to know.

We must have fallen asleep in this way, side by side, a gentle breeze caressing our naked forms, because the next thing I remember is being unkindly wakened by great draughts of water being flung against our bodies. Motsqueh and I stirred to find Cayuse Jem and Chuslum in our swimming hole and splashing us again and again by making great swipes with their arms through the water. After our initial shock, we boys decided turnabout was fair play and jumped into the pool to return the favor to our menfolk by splashing them with as much water as our decidedly smaller arms could muster.

We splashed and played and laughed, and I felt as though the earth had been created only for the four of us, for this odd little family that had been melded together here in the backwoods of a territory far away from what I had once thought was the only world that mattered. And we laughed and played until the menfolk grabbed us in their arms and held us and kissed us and kissed us some more, pinning our lean forms against the grassy bank of the pool. And as our backs were pressed into the taller grass of the bank, and as our ankles were raised toward heaven, and as our men prepared to perform the great act of male love right there, on the banks of our swimming pool, I gazed at Motsqueh, and Motsqueh gazed back at me, and he reached out and took my hand in his own. And as the sound of splashing water was replaced by the din of grunting, straining men and yelping, happy boys, and as Motsqueh squeezed my hand in both solidarity and joy, I turned my gaze to the heavens and gave thanks to whatever deity might bless such an ecstatic moment. And I prayed that this moment, this feeling, this palpable and overwhelming sense of love I felt from and for all three of these men, might never end. Even as I knew in the back of my mind it must, even as I knew summer would irrevocably and cruelly turn to autumn and that my father would recall me once more, even as I knew the arc of my life had already been knitted from fabric colder and more remote than the intense love and life I had come to know with Cayuse Jem, I still prayed and still gave thanks, for, indeed, in that moment, I had much to pray and give thanks for.

I must also confess, with some small twinge of embarrassment, that I snuck a rather prolonged glance at Chuslum as he mounted Motsqueh. And I must say, if anything, I think my good friend was under reporting the length and span of Chuslum's manhood. Frankly, it seemed less an appendage and more a third arm. Good heavens. It is a wonder the lad can walk at all.

31 August 1888

I FEEL OBLIGATED to note that—as I read over the previous entries in my little journal—I fear these recollections of mine have devolved from a serious meditation on my life into a rustic, masculine version of Mr. Cleland's *Fanny Hill*. I hasten to add I have never actually read the aforementioned book myself—Hardwicke was rather infamous in some circles for circulating a copy amongst the residential halls at Harvard, but I never had any strong inclination to peruse it for myself. I suppose I now comprehend why that is. Still, I admit myself somewhat red faced by the rather bawdy nature of these last few entries. Nonetheless, this journal is for me and me alone and is designed to be an accurate representation, not only of my life, but also of my current state of mind—thus, I suppose it is safe to say where both my life and my state of mind are, at least for the time being.

I do not think I should find myself lamenting this development in these pages anytime soon.

5 September 1888

I HAVE BECOME rather proficient in riding Boadicea at a cantor's pace, and today we successfully galloped for at least half of a mile before turning back toward home. Cayuse Jem is pleased with my progress, though he cautions me it is important to not grow ahead of my own pace and reminded me that Boadicea deserves at least half of the credit.

"I would wager that she deserves two-thirds of the credit, sir," I replied.

"Why is that, boy?"

"Four of the six legs involved belong to her, after all."

It is a good thing Cayuse Jem loves me for who I am, for I would never win the man with my sense of humor.

And yet while my skills as an equestrian grow, it has become evident to both Cayuse Jem and myself that I have absolutely no facility in training the horses for show. I cannot command a horse's attention the way Cayuse Jem can; I cannot persuade the animal into moving its foreleg in any particular manner. Indeed, I have no proficiency in cajoling a horse to do much of anything, which leads me to believe that Boadicea deserves more than two-thirds credit for any success I have demonstrated in riding.

Cayuse Jem and I spoke of this last night, as he held me in his arms.

"What does it matter, boy?" he asked me, kissing my forehead in a consolatory manner.

"I only wish to be of use to you, sir," I replied.

"You are of great use to me, boy. More than you can ever know."

"Yes, cooking, cleaning, I am of use there. Any good housekeeper could do the same."

Cayuse Jem squeezed his arms around me tighter. "Is that all you think I need you for, boy?"

"No, sir, of course not," I said. I understood what Cayuse Jem was saying, and I believed him, too. Yet still I felt glum, and something nagged at my soul, though what it was, I could not say.

"Boy," Cayuse Jem said, "remember when we talked, some time back, about the nature of a thing?"

"Yes, sir."

"It simply isn't your nature to train horses, boy. You have no desire for it. It's not you."

"But it *is* you, sir," I replied. "And I wish—"

"You wish what, boy?" Cayuse Jem said. "To be me?"

I did not know how to respond to his questions, because, quite frankly, I did not know what I wished for myself at all, save for one very vital thing. "I wish to love you, sir," I said, burrowing myself deeper into his arms.

"Aye, boy, and that you do better than any other in the wide world." And without another word Cayuse Jem used his great arms to twist me around in the bed, pinning me down and allowing me to demonstrate, for the second time that evening, just how deep my love for him ran.

10 September 1888

IT IS LATE, dreadfully late, but I find myself incapable of even closing my eyes, let alone achieving any actual rest or sleep. I should think I may never sleep again, given what has transpired today and the heavy concern that grips my heart; and yet I am in wonder that I do not sleep, considering the weariness in my bones and the exhausted condition of each of my limbs. It is my mind, truly, that can find no respite nor rest, and for that reason, I am heartened I thought to bring my little journal with me.

The day began gloomy and overcast; rain threatened, though Cayuse Jem thought this a good omen, given the generally dry conditions that have plagued us this summer. The little creek that provides water for the horses and the house is running low, and a good quantity of rain is necessary to replenish our stocks. And yet this gloom brought with it the foresight of great prescience, for a gloom has come over my heart in such a way that I fear I shall never know any other emotion, save the heavy dullness of apprehension and the dread of what may happen next.

Perhaps it is best I should start at the beginning.

I was completing my morning chores in the barn when I saw Chuslum at a distance, standing deathly still at the edge of the forest. Though the man's countenance is usually stagnant and subdued, no matter the occasion, today it had a pallor that disquieted me at once. Furthermore, I was taken aback by the immobility of his condition; he neither moved toward us nor advanced out of the shadow of the woods, but only stood deathly still.

I could tell, even from such a distance, something terrible was amiss.

Immediately, I dropped the shovel and ran for Cayuse Jem, who was busy exercising the horses. When Cayuse Jem saw Chuslum, it was evident by the look on his face that he, too, sensed something was very wrong. He advanced toward Chuslum, but the Indian held up his hands to prevent Cayuse Jem from approaching him, even though there was nearly half a furlong between them.

Chuslum spoke to Cayuse Jem in a raised voice. The Nez Perce language was never musical to my ears—not like French or Italian might seem—but to hear it shouted across an empty plain sent a chill directly to my soul. I could tell by the stiffening in Cayuse Jem's body that something terrible was indeed wrong, that some grave and awful misfortune had befallen the Indian village.

My first thought was of Motsqueh, of my good friend, and his absence in this scene did not dispel my disquietude in regard to his safety. I then wondered if perhaps my father's men had returned, and in force this time; we had heard no gunplay, but the small sliver of land I had ceded to the Indians for their use was some distance from here, and such sounds might not carry over the valley.

I steeled myself for whatever news might come. If it was my father's men, then I was determined to help. The Indians were on my land, not his, and if it came to it, I would stand up to my father and force him to cease his harassment of the Indians. Or, yes, I could sell the land to Old Man Peterson—with the condition, of course, that it be left available for use by the Indians as best they see fit. I could not imagine Mr. Peterson would be pleased to have Indians camping on his land, but the loss of such territory to his hated neighbor would surely upset my father to no end, which I felt could be enough to tempt Mr. Peterson to see things my way. Indeed, the more I thought on it, the more the plan made perfect sense to me. Eager to solve our friends' problem, I clutched Cayuse Jem by his arm and interrupted his conversation with Chuslum.

"I will sell the land to Mr. Peterson," I blurted out hastily. "Then my father's men will be forced to withdraw. They will have no choice. He will have no claim on it whatsoever, even by blood. And then Chuslum and his people—"

"It is not your father's men," Cayuse Jem interrupted quietly, a solemn timbre echoing in his voice.

I did not like the tenor of Cayuse Jem's words. "Then what is it, sir?"

"Typhoid."

Typhoid! I drew back my breath hastily; involuntarily, my hand sprang to my lips, and a question leapt into my mind.

"Motsqueh?"

Cayuse Jem spoke something to Chuslum, and I saw the Indian gravely nod his head.

"What can we do, sir?" I asked, bating my breath in horror and dismay.

Cayuse Jem shook his head. "I'm afraid there's little we can do, boy," he replied. "Chuslum has come to warn us to stay out of the forest, lest we get sick, and to ask for any supplies we can spare."

I shook my head. That was not enough. There must be more we could do, for Chuslum, for Motsqueh, for their people. But typhoid! I know little of the disease myself, save that it is deadly. On rare occasion, it would surface in some of the poorer districts in Boston; many would die. It never came to Cambridge or to any corner of the city the students from Harvard might visit, so I had never much to fear from typhoid; because of this, I knew precious little about the disease in general. Indeed, I had never much fascination with the natural sciences, though I had done well in my biology and chemistry courses in school. It was always books that held my sway, books that interested me—

A sudden thought—an inspiration—a wild idea—blazed into my brain. Without a word I ran from Cayuse Jem's side and back into the house.

Books. That was the answer, a book. Amongst the books I had purchased from Mr. Mackey was a pharmacopoeia. I had been reading it in the evenings, so that I might understand more about the treatment of ailments in case of emergent circumstances. I had remembered seeing within its pages—I was thumbing through them like a madman desperate to maintain some grasp on the flimsiest thread of his sanity—there! An entire chapter on nervous fever, also known as typhoid fever. The book talked quite extensively about its causes, about its symptoms and—a glimmer of hope—about a treatment for the disease.

I hastily scanned the pages. Much of what the book called for I knew the Indians would not have in their little village. But some of it could be made from the land, and we had small provision here in the house. The manor house would have even more. Clutching the book, I ran back to Cayuse Jem and to Chuslum as quickly as I could.

Both men were curious by my actions, though for very different reasons. I could discern from the look on Cayuse Jem's face he was worried for my emotional state; but Chuslum saw something in my face that he had not thought on until now—he saw hope.

"Sir," I sputtered between great pants, doing my best to catch my breath as the words tumbled out of me, "here, here, it talks all about it. It will help. It can help the Indians." As I was speaking, I held the book out before me, as if somehow its presence would clearly communicate that which I seemed incapable of doing at the moment.

"Calm down, boy," Cayuse Jem said, placing a soothing hand on my shoulder. "Tell me what you are saying, slowly."

"This book, here," I said, holding out the text before me, "is a pharmacopoeia." I could tell the word was meaningless to him, so I tried a different tack. "This is a medical book," I said. "It has a whole chapter in here on typhoid fever."

"I'm not sure how a book can help now, boy."

"No, sir, it can, truly. It talks about how the disease progresses, how to treat it, how to prevent it from spreading—I know it can help, sir. I know it can."

As we conversed, Chuslum waited impatiently, likely wondering what it was we were speaking about so animatedly. Finally, we heard him shout, but Cayuse Jem hesitated to say anything to him. "Are you sure this will help, boy?" he said. "A lot of these books are just nonsense and bunkum."

I shook my head. "Not this one, sir. Honest. It was published in Chicago only two years ago and has the latest in scientific findings. It was compiled and written by actual medical doctors." I paused for a moment, saying a silent prayer I was right. "I know it will help, sir."

Still hesitant, Cayuse Jem raised his voice and explained to Chuslum about the pharmacopoeia and how it might assist his people.

"We can send to the manor house for supplies," I said to Cayuse Jem, who translated to Chuslum for me. "Cheevers will give them to me without any questions. Well, a few, perhaps, but he will do it. We can drop the supplies in the woods. So long as we don't have actual contact with anyone who is sick, we cannot catch the disease."

The two men spoke, and for a moment Chuslum seemed buoyed by my plan. But then I saw his countenance grow dark again. He shouted something at Cayuse Jem, and even though there was great distance between him and us, I could swear I saw a bitter tear fall from the Indian's eye. I felt my heart cleave in twain just to see it.

"What is it, sir?" I asked. "What does he say?"

Cayuse Jem's voice was as gentle as possible, given the circumstances. "There's no one in the village who can read English, boy," he said. "The book is useless to them."

What I said next I uttered without thought, without consideration, without anything more conscious or intentional than human instinct itself.

"Then I must go, sir."

The words surprised me as much as Cayuse Jem, but I knew as soon as I expressed them it was the only way. And yet the thought of it filled me with a wholly new sensation, a palpable sense of fear that, for the moment, rendered me incapable of movement or even of speech. Still, I simply knew what I had spoken was true: I must be the one to go.

"Absolutely not." Cayuse Jem's response was as instinctual as my own, and much more forceful.

"I must, sir."

"No." Cayuse Jem's voice had stirred; never before had he raised his voice to me, though the emotion that quavered in his words was not anger. "I will not put you in danger, boy." He swallowed hard. "I will go."

I sadly shook my head. "You cannot read the text any more than the Indians, sir," I mournfully replied.

"You are teaching me to read, boy."

"Yes, sir, and you have made remarkable progress. But the book is too technical to be understood by one who is simply a beginner at reading."

"Then you will dictate to me what to do. Tell me now, and I shall go forward—"

But this was not possible, and Cayuse Jem knew so. "It is pages and pages, sir. It is too much to remember."

Cayuse Jem straightened up. I could see pain crossing his face, and how it pained me to know that my own actions—selfless though they may be—had placed it there. "Then I will go with you, boy."

"No, sir, you cannot do this. You must stay here and tend to the horses."

"You do not speak the Indian tongue, boy. How will you communicate to them what to do?"

This was an impediment I had not foreseen. But my scrambling brain quickly posed a solution. "Ask Chuslum if there is someone in the village who does understand English." Cayuse Jem refused to either move or speak. But I would not surrender this point. "Ask him." I softened my tone. "Please, sir."

Cayuse Jem shouted my question across the expanse that gulfed Chuslum from us, and I did not need him to translate the brief affirmative reply we received.

"You must stay here, sir," I said. "You must send word to Cheevers, to the manor house, and gather supplies and get them to us. You must tend to the horses. They need you."

There was no reasonable argument to make, but the feelings that passed between Cayuse Jem and myself were beyond reason. "I do not wish to lose you, boy," Cayuse Jem said, and I could see the vestiges of tears forming in his russet-brown eyes. "I have only just found you."

"I do not wish to be lost, sir." My own face was visibly streaked with tears, and yet, somehow, almost inexplicably, in amongst my tangible fear over what was to come, my heart was filled with tremendous affection and joy. "I love you, sir," I whispered to Cayuse Jem. The large man held me most tenderly in his arms, and I sobbed in both trepidation and elation. "If something should happen to me—"

"Don't say that, boy, you must never speak like that—"

"If it should, sir, I want you to know, I do not do this to hurt you. I do this because—because it is the type of man you are teaching me to be." As I said it, I knew it to be true. "Because it is what you would do, if you could. Because it is what we do in love. And that is what you have taught me, sir, above everything else."

"I love you, boy," Cayuse Jem whispered in my ear. His arms held me so fiercely I worried I might break a rib, though I wished him never to let me go. "Promise you will come back to me."

I nodded but said nothing, knowing I never wanted to utter any promise to Cayuse Jem I could not guarantee I would be able to keep. Instead, I finally pulled myself from the man's embrace and moved back to the house to gather what supplies I could.

As I collected the scant items we had that might aid in my upcoming endeavors, I could hear Cayuse Jem and Chuslum conversing loudly back and forth. I knew the Nez Perce word for "no" and heard it shouted several times, but, in the end, it seemed Cayuse Jem convinced Chuslum that my plan was the only way help might be found. My heart surged at this. The brave man was confronted with the grave illness of his own beloved, and yet he still did not wish to endanger me in any way, even if that meant further endangering his own boy. But I was glad Cayuse Jem was able to convince Chuslum of our plan. I knew it was the only way to save Motsqueh.

In the end, so did Chuslum.

Cayuse Jem had saddled Boadicea for me, and he placed our meager supplies into saddle bags as I prepared to depart. "Take this to Cheevers," I said, handing him a note, "and then bring the supplies. When you get near the village, fire your gun twice in the air, so we will know it is you. You must not come into the village, no matter how much you may wish to do so." I held Cayuse Jem's gaze in my own. "Promise me this, sir."

Cayuse Jem nodded, and then it was his turn to elicit promises of his own. "Boy," he started, then added "Nat"—I knew his use of my name only underscored the seriousness of his words—"you must promise me that you will not tend to the sick yourself. Do you understand? You must keep distant from them. You can give direction, but you will not tend to them yourself. Do you give me your word?"

I knew he would not let me leave if I did not agree and loved him all the more for it. "Yes, sir."

"And mind Chuslum," he added. "If he tells you to do something, do it. That includes telling you to get on your horse and come back home at once. You will not question him, as you would not question me in a matter like this. Do you understand?" Cayuse Jem's instructions indicated to me he had reached an understanding with our Indian friend; that explained, perhaps, the loud conversation I had overheard. But I nodded at this as well.

Cayuse Jem engulfed me in his arms one last time. There seemed nothing more to say, so we said nothing. Our arms and our aspects said it all. Then I climbed on to Boadicea and, with a gentle prod of my heels, steered her toward Chuslum, toward the Indian village, and away from Cayuse Jem.

Chuslum led the horse through the woods, while I stayed mounted, devouring every word the pharmacopoeia spoke on the subject of typhoid fever. I was unsure to what extent the disease had spread, or what stage it might be in. I wanted to be prepared to begin helping as soon as I arrived at the Indian village.

And yet I was wholly unprepared for what I saw as the village came into view. Perhaps it was the word "village" and all the connotations of stability and civility that accompanied the term; or perhaps it was my friendship with Motsqueh and Chuslum that allowed me to cling to the delusion that their lives outside of our time together must be as storied and idyllic as my own had become. But it was evident, just from one glance at this wretched space, that the situation for these people was desperate long before any sickness had arrived.

I reminded myself that this settlement was new; that these people had been displaced from their previous home and forced to settle here, all against their wills. It explained the precious few possessions they had, and the lack of sturdy domiciles. The Indians were living in tents, simple structures that were easy to dissemble and reassemble at a moment's notice. There was water nearby, true, a small branch of the same creek that serviced Cayuse Jem and his ranch; and the woods surely had plenty game. But there were no crops, and little by way of necessary stores. I shuddered to imagine what the harsh Idaho winter would be like for these people.

There were perhaps a shade less than forty people there in total, ranging in age from a few years to a ripe old dotage indeed. There seemed more women than men. They viewed me suspiciously. I presumed their interactions with white people had been, for the most part, less than favorable. And yet, I supposed if I were to meet them under pleasanter circumstances, I would find each member of the tribe as earthy and amiable and full of life as Motsqueh and Chuslum.

Motsqueh. The thought of my friend spurred me forward. If I could help these people, I must.

Chuslum spoke to his people. It was clear by the way they marked him that he was a leader among his tribe. I presumed he was telling them I had come to help. I hoped so, anyway. I only wished, as fervently as I could, that I could bring succor and aid to these villagers. Then Chuslum brought me to the only English speaker in the settlement, a woman whose age, I surmised, surpassed my own by only a few years. "You speak English, yes?" I asked her.

"Oh, yes, sir," she replied.

For a moment her use of the titular "sir" made me smile and think of Cayuse Jem; but there was important work to do, and I set about it right away. "Please, ask the villagers if any of them have had this disease before, at some point in the past?"

The young woman turned to the village and repeated my question. There seemed some confusion, so she repeated it again. At this several individuals stepped forward. There were five women and three men in total, including Chuslum, all over thirty years in age.

"Please, sir," the young Indian woman said, "there was, many years ago, sickness in the tribe. Many in the village died, but these people survived." She hesitated before speaking again. "I, too, have had this sickness before."

I was impressed by the well of English the young woman possessed and wondered how she might have come by it, but there was little time to dwell on such matters now. "If you have had the sickness," I spoke, as my translator repeated my words, "you cannot become sick again with it. You are immune to the disease." I turned to my translator. "I'm sorry—I do not know your name."

"Josefina."

Josefina. It was certainly not an Indian name; at least it was not like any Indian name I had ever known. But the answer to this mystery would also have to wait. "Josefina, how many are ill? And where are they?"

Josefina consulted with another member of the tribe, an elderly woman, before turning back to me. "There are seven people who are stricken," she said. "They are in the tents." She indicated various teepee-like structures constructed out of sticks and animal hides. These were temporary domiciles, I supposed, hastily manufactured after the recent move.

The generally benign conditions of the summer would allow anyone to live, for a time, in such circumstances. But the pharmacopoeia indicated that dark, close quarters were conducive to the spread of the disease. "Josefina," I said, "we need to quarantine the people who are ill."

"I'm sorry, sir," she said. "I do not understand what is 'quarantine.'"

"We need to keep them away from everyone else. And they need to be in the open air. Josefina, instruct the villagers to set up a tent, over here," I said, pointing toward the northeast corner of the village. The flat land and long grass would make for the most comfortable space for the stricken to repose. "There needs to be a roof of some kind, to prevent rain, but no sides—the stricken need fresh air." Josefina nodded and relayed my instructions. "Make sure that no villager who has never had the sickness goes near anyone who is ill. They must be kept as separate as possible. Do you understand?" Josefina nodded again. "Only those who previously had typhoid can tend to the sick. They cannot become ill again. And they must limit their contact with anyone who is not sick. Is that clear, too?" Josefina nodded a third time and spoke some more words to the villagers.

"Water," I said. My mind was processing far more quickly than my mouth could speak; there was much to be done. "Josefina, assign four women to gather as many pots and water jugs as possible. They will draw water from the stream, but it must be boiled. Do you understand? No one— not anyone who is sick or well—can drink any water unless it has been boiled first."

I turned toward the source of water. "Send a few men upstream. Tell them to follow the water as far as they can. We have to find the source of the contamination."

"I'm sorry, sir," Josefina asked, "but what does this mean?"

I did my best to explain. "Typhoid fever is caused by feces in drinking water—at least that's the best guess for now."

"Feces?"

"Excrement." But this, too, also earned me a blank look. I was not sure how to explain, so I did my best to pantomime what I meant. Josefina finally nodded in understanding. It would have perhaps been a moment for hysterics, the young bibliophile, son of Jessum Goldsmith, pantomiming taking a shite in the woods to an Indian maid, had the situation not been so serious. "Have the men trace the water upstream. If we follow the water, we may find the source of the problem. It need not be human. It could be from a farm." My father had small farms dotted all over his land. There was no telling how many might intersect this stream. "See if they can find any obvious source of feces. Tell them to go as far as they can—two miles, at least. And for heaven's sake, tell them to be careful," I added, knowing most of the farmers in the area would not look kindly on Indians trespassing on their land.

By now the village had erupted into a sea of commotion. Perhaps the Indians felt a new optimism at my presence, or perhaps they simply responded well at having something to do in the face of a crisis of helplessness. The hospital tent was set up with great haste, and the sick hobbled over there as best they could and rested on blankets and mats. I was pleased to see that all of them were able to take to their feet, even Motsqueh, though the youth did not notice me as Chuslum aided him to his place in the makeshift infirmary.

I was less pleased to see that two of the ill were small children. I sighed, running my fingers through my dark hair. I prayed I knew what I was doing.

I called Josefina to me again. "We need to know the extent of the symptoms," I said to her, "to understand how far the disease has progressed." Among the survivors of the disease was a capable woman whose weathered face and wizened eyes suggested she might be some sixty years of age. I appointed her as head nurse and asked her to describe the symptoms of the sick. Josefina translated. "They have pain here," she said, pointing to the bowels, "and fever. They are weary and red in the face, and they have no wish to eat. And when they do eat, their passages are very loose." At this she blushed, but my questions were about to become far more personal.

"What color are they?" I asked.

Josefina was confused. "The people?"

I shook my head. "Their stool." She did not understand this word. What was the one she had used?—"Their passages."

She spoke with the old nurse, who confirmed that the stool was coming out yellowish-green. "Is there any blood?" I asked and was relieved when the old woman shook her head.

"Is the pain in the bowels more on one side?" I asked. Upon hearing my query, the old woman pointed to her right side.

"Is there a rash?" I asked. I turned to Josefina. "Have her check the stomach and torso of each person in the tent. Tell her to look for small red spots." Josefina translated my instructions, and the old woman hobbled off. When she came back, her report was negative. "Good," I said, breathing a heavy sigh of relief. The disease was still in an early stage. According to the pharmacopoeia, there may be time to stall its progress.

The old woman said something then, speaking to me more than to Josefina. "I'm sorry, sir," Josefina said, "but she wishes to know—are you a medicine man for your people?"

A medicine man. Was this what I had appointed myself, though I had no rights or training to claim such a title? "No," I said, as much to myself as to Josefina, "I am not a medicine man. I'm just a boy with a book." Josefina seemed unsure as to the ultimate meaning of these words, and so she left my comments untranslated and merely shook her head in response to the old Indian woman's query.

My mind clouded for a moment, consumed with doubt over the whole enterprise. I *was* just a boy with a book. Was I foolish to think I could do this? Was this arrogance, not philanthropy? Still, I had already begun this endeavor, and there was too much to do, including medicines to prepare, and thus no time to ruminate on my own purpose and intent. "Josefina, send some of the young people out to forage for peppermint. Is it too early for grapes? Ask them to find some wild grapes as well." I looked around the village, but there were no plantings anywhere. "Josefina, is there rhubarb available anywhere?"

She shook her head. "What do the Indians take for constipation?" She shook her head again, clearly confused by the word "constipation." I held my hand in front of my bowels. "When they cannot make passages?" I reiterated, a hint of question in my voice.

"Black root," she said.

"Gather as much as you can. If anyone's bowel becomes blocked, we can use it to help. There is a small amount of barley on my horse. Have some of the women prepare barley water." I was pleased to see the village did have a small number of chickens. "The eggs will be useful when people begin to recover. Josefina, is there any milk?" She shook her head. We would have to do without the milk, then. I had one last instruction for her. "There is corn meal on the horse as well. Have a gruel prepared." That was it. There was nothing more I could do until Cayuse Jem arrived with the quinine and bismuth. I only hoped the note I wrote for Cheevers reached him in time.

Each of us set out to work, to complete our appointed task as swiftly as we could. The village was struck with quiet, a quiet that was intermittently interrupted by the moans of the sick.

I took a moment to observe the scene. I turned my eyes upward, attempting to tell the time of day based on the progress of the sun. It was far more difficult to do here, in a clearing in the woods, than in the more wide-open spaces of Cayuse Jem's ranch. My best guess was that it was midafternoon, around 3:00. I had left Cayuse Jem less than four hours ago, and yet, somehow, it seemed much longer. As long as a lifetime, perhaps.

I felt myself fall backward, bracing myself against a nearby tree, before crumpling to the ground. I felt both worn out and oddly giddy at the same time. Still, I took but a brief recess to gather my thoughts. There was much work to be done, preparing medications and boiling water and making food for both the sick and the healthy. And besides, like the Indians, I found it best to keep busy, so that I would not dwell upon all the things that worried me most.

It was perhaps three hours later when we heard the sharp retort of gunfire—one shot, then two. Cayuse Jem! Most of the villagers looked frightened at the sound—I had neglected to mention our prearranged signal to them—but Chuslum understood what it meant and took off in a flash. I longed to go myself, but at best I would only catch a glimpse of Cayuse Jem, and I figured to see him—to see him without being able to speak with him, to be held by him—would only cause me pain. So I stayed where I might do some good.

Chuslum soon returned with a bundle that included, as an answer to my prayers, quinine and bismuth. There was also a small folded piece of paper that Chuslum handed to me. I unfolded it, but saw there were no words on it, only a crudely drawn heart.

I folded the paper and put it in my breast pocket, Cayuse Jem's heart close to my own.

Now that we had quinine and bismuth, we could begin a pharmaceutical regimen for the stricken. Cloth cooled in peppermint water would help tamp down the fevers, and the pharmacopoeia recommended a poultice made of lobelia, one that had to be replenished frequently, to aid the pain in the bowels. I did not know what lobelia was, but, thankfully, the pharmacopoeia included both glossary and index, and the description for lobelia included several of the plant's other names. Here in the territory it was known as Indian pink, and this time of year, there was plenty growing on the edges of the forest. I sent two of the Indians to gather as much as they could.

The ill were given barley water, by mouth, several spoonfuls every hour. This was supplanted by sweet juice from the grapes. When their appetites returned, they could move on to the corn meal gruel. All the stricken were given bismuth to abate their symptoms and tincture of quinine to boost their strength; the latter I also gave to everyone in the village, myself included, to prevent the further spread of the fever. We had enough for two, perhaps three days at most. I only hoped Cheevers minded my note, and Cayuse Jem received another shipment of the necessary drug soon.

The entire village dedicated itself to fighting the sickness. Groups of women took turns boiling vast quantities of water, until every pot, jug, and cup in the village was full. The liquid regimen outlined in the pharmacopoeia called for hourly care, and the poultices required constant replenishing. But the nursemaids worked unceasingly, and without complaint, dividing their duties and tending to the ill as if each was their most tender loved one.

About an hour after sunset the scouting party returned. One of the three men had grown sick during their sojourn, and I cursed myself that I had not foreseen this possibility. He was taken to the infirmary, and the other two men I quarantined on the far side of the encampment. The ill man was immediately cared for, while the two scouts were given quinine in what I hoped was a preventative measure.

Their efforts had borne fruit, however. They reported that some ways upstream—a bit less than half of a mile, from what I gathered—there was a small farm. The farmer possessed a large pile of animal dung—taken from pigs and cows and used on his vegetables, no doubt. The pile was kept near a crook of the stream. The farm must pull its water from above the dung pile; otherwise, they would have shown symptoms of illness before this, and if there had been any sickness in the area, Cayuse Jem and I would be sure to hear about it. But this could be the source of the fever in the Indians, newly arrived as they were to this spot. The contaminant must diffuse as it travels through the water (which might explain why many of the Indians had so far escaped symptoms of the disease), but still, enough is reaching them to cause a problem.

The scouts reported that they tramped another two miles or so up the stream and saw no other sign of contamination. Fixing this source of contamination was crucial to solving this crisis. I said to Chuslum—through Josefina—that we must send Cayuse Jem to speak to the farmer. He would be able to convince him to move the dung. I was eager to send someone right away, but Chuslum said no. Looking around, he could see that exhaustion had settled in on the entire village. It would be better, he said, to start fresh in the morning.

I realized he was right, and I remained mindful of my pledge to Cayuse Jem that I must obey Chuslum, whatever command he gave. And, indeed, I was exhausted. But sleep would not come when I lay my head down, and nor, it seems, will it come now, even though I have writ my day's story down in my little journal. Indeed, I find even as I write this, the dread that has been omnipresent in the back of my mind threatens to move to the forefront. I have done what I thought was right, and I have followed the pharmacopoeia as adroitly as possible—but I am no doctor. I have no training in this field whatsoever. As Cayuse Jem says, a man must follow his nature. But my nature has never bent to science, only to books, and I could not help but feel a fool playing with things he ought not. Could I truly help these people? Or was I dooming them, along with myself? Would we all succumb to the fever before this was over?

Perhaps it was the lateness of the hour, or the weariness of my bones, but a more unsettling, disconcerting question darted into my mind, one that I had been avoiding since I arrived in the Indian village so many hours ago.

Would I ever see Cayuse Jem again?

11 September 1888

I AWOKE BEFORE dawn, which indicated to me that, at some point during the night, I must have fallen asleep. The little village lay quiet. Four of the nursemaids were tending to the patients, including Chuslum. I had sent the other four to bed before I retired. It would be important to do everything we could to keep the healthy from becoming ill themselves, and that included staving off exhaustion with regular sleep.

I knew, though, that I would have little luck in ordering Chuslum to bed. I doubted he had slept at all, too anxious to leave Motsqueh's side unless it was absolutely necessary. At least today would be quieter; with the infirmary set, with pots upon pots of water boiled and the medicines prepared, all that was left now was to wait, wait for more medicine to be delivered, wait to see if anyone else fell ill, wait to see if the fever could be stalled, or if it would advance in its progress.

I lay still for a moment, huddled on my bed of white pine boughs. There was also, of course, the question of sanitation. At first dawn I would send a runner to Cayuse Jem, to ascertain if he might be able to persuade the farmer to move his pile of dung. But the more I thought on it, the more I believed it best the Indians move their own sanitation area as well. Perhaps I was simply erring on the side of caution; or perhaps I believed that giving the healthy the chore of digging a new trench system would keep them from losing their minds with worry.

I rose from my makeshift bed and moved closer to one of the burning fires. A woman tending the logs shifted to one side, to make room for me, but I waved her off with my hand and a weary smile; for the moment, I preferred to stand.

I saw a figure approaching me, cup in hand. It was Josefina. She handed me a hot, dark concoction. "Tea," she explained, and I brought the warm liquid to my lips. I winced at the bitterness of the flavor. This was not Asian tea, but some local infusion, probably made from tree bark. I took another sip and wondered briefly when a morsel of food had last passed my lips.

Josefina saw my reaction to the drink. "Yes, sir, it does take some getting used to," she said with a smile. "It took me some time as well. But, with the grace of God, all things are possible."

There was something in the manner in which she spoke, in the way she constructed her words, in the simple and sincere expression of faith she had used. "Are you a Christian?" She nodded. "And you are not Nez Perce, are you?" I asked.

Josefina shook her head. "My people are from Mexico," she said.

"That explains your name," I replied, "and your faith. Tell me, how did you come to be here?"

Josefina fell to her knees and then reclined on the back of her heels. I had seen many Indian women do this in the village; apparently, they found it comfortable. I confess I found the stance less so, and I ended up sitting on the forest floor in a rather ungainly style, finally ending up with my back propped against a tree. "I was born in Mexico," she began, "or so I was told. I do not remember it. When I was young, my parents moved my brothers and me to Texas, to live with many other *mezistos*, and to work on a big ranch there."

I took another sip of the tea, settling in to listen to her story. "When I am seven, a great sickness came to our camp. Typhoid. We were all very ill. Many died, including my whole family."

"I am so sorry," I murmured.

Josefina gave me a wan smile. "It was many years ago," she said. "Sometimes, it seems even longer. But I remember them all so well. I remember my father's voice, and my mother dancing. How she loved to dance."

She fell into the silence of recollection. "How did you come to be here, in Idaho?" I prodded.

"One of the men from the ranch brought me and other children north. When we arrived, he sold us one by one, to work in the fields, or as servants in the home."

"That's terrible."

Josefina shrugged. "I was lucky. I was bought by the family of an old woman who wanted a girl to sweep her floor and keep her company. I remember the first time I saw her. She had great billowing mounds of snowy-white hair. Never have I seen such a thing! I had heard of a snowman in Texas—though of course I had never seen one—and I asked her if she was a snow lady." Josefina smiled at the memory. "Fortunately for me, when my words were translated to her, she laughed, and loudly too! Oh yes, she was a good spirit, my Madame." Seeing my puzzled expression, Josefina hastened to explain. "Madame was what I was told to call her. I did not know why. For many years I thought this to be an English term, and I called every woman I met Madame! It is only later that I learn her husband was French, from Canada."

"And Madame is the one who taught you English?"

Josefina nodded. "Yes, and I taught her a little Spanish, mostly songs and poems. It was just the two of us, for many years, but it was pleasant enough. And then, one day, her heart gave out. And I was alone again."

"When was that?" I asked.

"Four years ago. I was seventeen. I tried to get work as a servant girl. I can cook and clean and sew. But the people around here... They see *mezistos* in the same way they see the Indians. Not as people at all." I could only nod at this, imagining how our family housekeeper would react at a girl from Mexico looking for work at the manor house. I wondered, in fact, if Josefina had looked for work at the manor house and was turned away. It was the largest house for many miles; for a girl in her situation, it may have made sense to try her luck there. The thought of our housekeeper turning Josefina away disturbed me immensely, but Josefina was still talking, and I pushed such notions from my mind and focused on her words instead. "I was alone for many days and nights. I was hungry and scared. But then the Nez Perce took me in. We always knew they were in the woods, Madame and I. Madame never said a word when they placed snares to catch rabbits and squirrels for their stewpots on her property. Madame hated squirrels with a passion, so I imagine she felt they were doing her a great service." Josefina gave a low laugh. "And when I was turned out of my home, they took me in and were very kindly to me. Soon I was married to one of them."

"You are married?" I said. "I should like to meet your husband. Where is he?"

Josefina somberly nodded her head in the direction of the makeshift infirmary. "I am so sorry, Josefina," I said. I frowned and took another sip of the tea. In all my time yesterday spent barking orders and treating Josefina as my assistant, I had never considered the feelings of the person who was assisting me. I felt ashamed at this oversight.

She bit her lip. "Sir, please, may I ask you a question?"

"Of course, Josefina."

"It has been three moons since I have had my courses," she began. There were small dots of red on her cheeks as she spoke, but the bewildered look upon my face made it evident I did not understand to what she was referring. She placed her hand upon her stomach and tried again. "I am to have a child, I should think," she said. "Please, is my baby safe from the fever?"

"I do not know, Josefina," I said, blurting out an answer without thinking. Immediately, I felt chagrined. It would have been much wiser to consult the pharmacopoeia first, or at least couch my language in such a way as to provide the woman a sense of hope, instead of letting her remain worried and concerned. "What I mean to say," I hastily added, "is that I am no expert in—women's affairs. But I should think, as you are immune to the disease, that your baby would also be safe." What I said held a certain logic, and as I spoke it, I became convinced it was at least a plausible reply. Had I but thought first before I spoke, I might not have added to the considerable apprehension that already bedeviled all of us.

But Josefina herself seemed to have a different reaction. She reached over and took my hand in hers. "God has sent you to us," she said. "I believe it is for a reason, sir."

"Josefina, you need not call me sir," I said. "I am your peer by age, and frankly, I do not think the word suits me at all."

"What shall I call you then?" she asked.

"You may call me—" I began but then interrupted myself. I almost told her to call me "boy;" clearly I had become quite accustomed to answering to that designation. But that would hardly do here. "Nathanial—Nat," I finally finished. "My name is Nat."

"Nat?" There was something in the name that seemed familiar to her. "Are you Tiptip?" she asked me. "Motsqueh's friend?"

"Has he spoken of me?" I am unsure why this news surprised me, but it did.

Josefina smiled. "He speaks of little else!" she said. "Tiptip, his great learned friend, his friend who loves his books. He speaks of you quite often. And yes, you are our benefactor, are you not? It was you who brought us to this land, yes?"

"For all the good it did," I muttered. "I think perhaps this land may be cursed."

Josefina nodded solemnly. "That is a belief among the Indians too. But in Mexico, we do not believe that land is bad. Only people are bad."

I gave Josefina an appreciative glance. "There is great wisdom in what you say." Over the tree line I could see the first rays of the sun rising in the east. I looked around and saw that the people of the village had begun to stir. "I only hope you are correct," I added.

The old Indian woman came over to us then and spoke in halting tones to Josefina. "Another member of the village grew sick in the night," Josefina translated. "She is asking if they should move her to be with the others."

"Yes," I said, nodding. "If anyone grows sick, move them immediately. And have her check all of the patients closely. Let me know if any new symptoms appeared in the night."

The old woman shuffled off to perform her task. I signaled one of the scouts from the previous day to join us. "Josefina, tell him he must go to Cayuse Jem and deliver a message for me." Quickly I reported that Cayuse Jem must be sent to the farmstead and ask the people there to move their dung pile. "And make sure he does not leave the tree line," I said to Josefina. "Have him stand silent and wait. Tell him not to approach the house under any circumstances." I could not bear the thought of Cayuse Jem becoming ill. "Cayuse Jem will be looking for him and will know what to do." Josefina translated my message to the scout, who departed with a brisk nod and nary a word.

I would have preferred to send Chuslum to Cayuse Jem, but I was not sure the Indian would agree to leave Motsqueh's side again, and I did not wish to ask such a great favor from him unless it was absolutely necessary. Besides, I felt it important he try to get some rest, even though I felt sure that Chuslum, like myself, would find sleep a fleeting partner at best.

The old nursemaid was shuffling over to us and quickly reported her findings to Josefina. "Most of the sick have shown no change, but in three of them there are new symptoms," Josefina relayed to me.

"What is it?" I asked, a sinking feeling cascading through my stomach.

"There is the rash," Josefina explained. "Also, the mouth and tongue are very dry. And there is a blackness on the tongue, a—how you say?—a coating."

This was ill tidings indeed. But I knew it was imperative not to show my concern to the Indians. "Josefina, please tell them to maintain our course for now, to give the medicines as ordered and to ensure that all of the stricken are to continue taking liquid. Do you understand?" Josefina nodded. "I must consult my book," I added, turning away from her and moving toward the saddlebag where I was keeping the pharmacopoeia and my journal.

I turned to the book as a source of hope and an act of faith, but I already knew what it was going to say. Still, I read the passages on typhoid fever again and again, hoping to find something—*anything*—I had missed the first twenty times I had read them.

I had come to understand the pharmacopoeia's central hypothesis in the treatment of the disease rather well. The liquid therapy, the need to ensure that the bowel kept moving—all was designed to cleanse the body, to purge it of the disease. Even the peppermint water would draw contaminants through the skin. If applied consistently, or so the book said, the fever could be halted in its progress.

And yet it was also clear by what was writ in the pharmacopoeia that, for three of the patients at least, the disease was progressing rapidly. This was an ill sign indeed. There was still the possibility of recovery, provided the stricken could continue to take liquids by mouth. That was important. If they should fall into a stupor, or if they should begin to vomit, the pharmacopoeia recommended injections of elixir of vitriol or a tincture of prickly ash-berries. There was no way for us to inject anyone, and we had no access to these medicines. Should that happen, it was all truly in God's hands.

I told Josefina to move the sickest members of the tribe to the far end of the infirmary tent, for all the good it would do. There was nothing else to be done for them.

All we could do now was wait.

And dig. I ordered new trenches put in place for sanitation purposes, as far removed from the camp as seemed prudent. The scout I sent to Cayuse Jem had returned, having relayed his message. Cayuse Jem had told him to return tomorrow at dawn for a reply.

That left only one directive for me to give. I sent Josefina to Chuslum to order him to bed.

He did not argue; he did not respond at all, Josefina told me. Finally, though, the entreaties of Josefina and the old woman I had placed in charge of the ill wore him down, and he left the tent to rest his head, at least for a short period of time.

As for me, I thought it prudent that I should do the same.

12 September 1888

THERE IS MUCH ill news to report. There was considerable rain last night, which has lasted well into today, and which has hampered the efforts to dig a new sanitation system. The rain forced the healthy members of the village to huddle together in several small tents. It also brought a chill to the air, requiring us to give up the remaining blankets to those stricken with the disease.

We are running low on necessary supplies, especially the quinine. I do not think we will have enough to last us the night.

There is plenty of food for the healthy members of the village, as the Indians are quite skilled at catching game, and know which native plants are good for eating. We are running low on cornmeal gruel, though, and will need more cornmeal soon.

Plus, the scout went to meet Cayuse Jem this morning as directed, but even after an hour's wait, Cayuse Jem did not appear.

There has been some good news. No other member of the village has come down with the sickness, and the disease is not advancing in any of those who have it. Still, the three whose symptoms are most advanced have shown no improvement, or so I am told.

And, worst of all, one of those three is Motsqueh.

Chipmunk! My friend, my brother... My heart ached for him, and for Chuslum as well. And yet that was all I was capable of doing to help him. I felt powerless before the advance of the disease.

Josefina told me that many in the village wish to leave. They fear falling ill themselves and believe this place to be cursed. Some of them whisper is it only a matter of time before they all succumb. So far the elders in the tribe, who have seen the disease before, have convinced them that leaving would compound their troubles. "But," Josefina added, "I do not know how long that will last." I shook my head. Without the work of every individual, I knew the stricken would not survive. And if any of the Indians left the village and carried the sickness with them into the world, there was no telling who they might infect.

This must be avoided at all costs. But I did not know how to prevent anyone from leaving, if they so wished it. I was just a boy with a book, after all.

I walked to one of the far corners of the encampment, where Boadicea has been kept. I have been neglecting her since I have arrived in the village. One of the men of the tribe has kindly looked after her, exercising her and ensuring she has fresh water and grass (happily, the pharmacopoeia reports animals cannot catch the disease, so I did not have to worry about that). In the thickest of the rain, he tied her to a white pine tree so that she was largely protected from the damp and the chill. I went to her, and she nuzzled my cheek worriedly. There was comfort in her touch, but it was cold comfort at best. How I longed instead to be with Cayuse Jem, on our farm, in his bed, warm and safe in the arms of the man I loved.

Instead, I buried my head into the side of Boadicea's neck and wept.

13 September 1888

THE ENTIRE VILLAGE was awakened today by the sound of gunfire. At first, a general panic threatened to sweep through the tribe, as trouble with settlers was surely the worst thing that could happen in this moment. But then the shot was repeated, and we realized the sounds were a signal from Cayuse Jem.

Bless the man I love! And bless Cheevers! Cayuse Jem has brought with him medicine—quinine and bismuth—cornmeal, and grain and vegetables and dried beef and more. He brought with him news, good news, that the farmer had moved his dung pile away from the stream. I calculated it would take time but, hopefully, with the improved sanitation, this would mean the village's water supply would remain safe.

I did not see him, of course, and I could only hope the Indians who spoke with Cayuse Jem told him I was safe. If Chuslum had gone, he could have conveyed my deep and abiding love, though I imagined his terms of endearment would be far more terse and gruff than my own.

There was further good news this afternoon—many of the stricken had found their appetites and were requesting more to eat than spoonfuls of cornmeal gruel and barley water. I had the cooks mix eggs into the gruel and told them to prepare beef broth with a few boiled vegetables. If their stools became more viscous in a day or so, then—according to the pharmacopoeia—they would fully recover.

The three patients whose disease had progressed the furthest, however, showed little sign of recovery. The group included an elderly woman, a small boy, and Motsqueh. My book told me that the disease was most deadly to small children and the elderly, and so I knew that the first two patients were in the most immediate danger. And yet my racing mind dwelt most upon Motsqueh, my friend, my brother. How I longed for us to be at our swimming hole again, laughing and playing without a care in the world. Was it only three weeks ago that we were there with our men, sealing our bonds of love side by side? It felt like a lifetime, like the life of a different person altogether, now.

Josefina brought me a bowl of the beef broth and vegetables, fortified with rabbit meat, and some of the flat Indian bread that the women cooked on large stones located next to the fire. "You must eat," she said. "You look thin, and pale—pale even for a white man."

I smiled at her levity and accepted the food graciously, though I had little stomach for it. I placed the bowl beside me on the forest floor and the flattened bread on top. I told Josefina that I was heartened her husband was recovering well. "He is very hungry indeed," she told me, "though, for him, that is his most natural state." She had earlier pointed him out to me, and I must confess, he was stouter than most Indians I had ever seen. But he had a pleasant face, and it was obvious Josefina was very fond of him. "I am happy to see him better," she said to me quietly, as if to show happiness over her good fortune might be disconcerting to some of the others, whose loved ones still suffered so cruelly. She craned her neck to peer at Chuslum, who was ever standing guard at Motsqueh's side. "They have deep feeling, those two," she said.

Emboldened by a lack of sleep and my growing respect for her, I said to Josefina, "You understand about those two, do you not? You understand that they—" I could not conceive of a delicate word that would complete the sentiment fitfully, so I left my sentence, and my meaning, hanging in the air.

"That they love?" Love. Of course. It was so simple, really, wasn't it? "Oh, yes. It is understood here. Some men are this way. And some women are, as well. You are, yes, are you not?" Her question surprised me, but I supposed, knowing Motsqueh as I do, that he would not keep this secret here, or, indeed, even see it as something to be kept secret. Still, outside of our little family...but I nodded and smiled shyly. Josefina smiled in return. "And you love this man...this Jim?"

"Jem. Cayuse Jem," I said. "And yes, I... I love him very much." I swallowed hard. "With all my heart."

Josefina placed her hand on my heart. Her touch was warm. There was something utterly powerful in this simple gesture of acceptance and understanding. "What we do from love, it must be a good thing, yes?" I was incapable of speech, moved as I was by the humanity being shown to me, so I merely nodded in reply. "The Nez Perce have a saying: if you love one member of a people, then you love all the people. This is why, in the past, so many conflicts were settled with marriage." She removed her hand from my heart. Her dark eyes twinkled with merriment. "Of course, this did not always work out for the best. And I often wonder how many times they asked the woman her opinion of the whole matter. After all, it is men who make quarrels, but it is women who make a marriage, and if she is wed against her wishes... Still, it is not such a bad way to do things, is it?"

"No, not at all."

Josefina took my hands in hers. "You came here because you love Motsqueh, and Chuslum. And therefore you love us all." She dropped my hands. "Or so the Nez Perce say." With a nod of her head, she indicated the bowl of food beside me. "Now eat." And as she stood and turned to walk away, I picked up the bread and the bowl, and then, hungry for the first time in many days, I began to eat.

14 September 1888

THE SICKNESS CLAIMED its first victim today. The elderly woman. I do not know her name. Her fever heightened greatly, and her bowels had ceased to move the previous evening. The preparation of black root proved no aid, and she was lost early this morning.

And I do not even know her name.

The mourning customs and practices of these people are unfamiliar to me, but I directed the body be buried immediately. The men were silent as they carried out this task; the women wailed, but it was a worn out, hollow sound, one borne not just from the honest and true sentiments of the bearers, but also from a weariness that threatened to sap the diminishing strength from us all.

I did not watch this practice, or participate in their mourning; it did not seem my place to do so. I know that, in days past, the Nez Perce buried their dead under mounds of dirt and grass. I did not know if it was the same now. I only knew that my heart ached at my great failure to save the wretched woman who was lost.

Yet the village is not without hope, either. Most of the sick are recovering, and there have been no new cases of the fever. Though the ill are still as weak as kittens, their fevers have abated; tomorrow, they can start to take small bites of bland food. And yet for Motsqueh and the little boy—whose name is Peopeo—there has been no improvement. As the village feels the chances for its own survival improving, it frets over the possible loss of two of its young sons. This mélange of optimism and dismay has paralyzed us all.

All we can do is wait on baited tenterhooks, I suppose, and pray to whatever gods might listen.

17 September 1888

I AM HOME now.

Though I do not remember the journey here.

That is not completely accurate. I remember bits and snatches of it. I rode Boadicea. It drizzled rain. And I clutched the pharmacopoeia and my journal to my chest, as if they were more precious than gold.

But I do not remember the trail, do not remember the shape of the branches we passed, do not remember the call of songbirds in the early morning air. I do remember the smell of the rain, but not the feel of it on my skin. I remember swaying gently as my beloved Boadicea carried me home, but I do not remember the sensation of her gravitas below me, or the feeling of safety once I had alit upon her back.

I was guided by two of the Indians, the brave scouts who first searched for signs of contamination. They knew the way. I was entrusted to their care. Perhaps it was fitting, since their lives—and so many others—had recently been entrusted to mine.

We had barely emerged from the woods when I saw Cayuse Jem coming toward us, running, moving as fast as he could carry his bulk and his might. I suppose I might laugh at such a sight, were it not an act of love and devotion and concern, and were I capable of such a thing at that moment.

I do not remember how I came down from the horse, or how long we waited by the edge of the woods for Cayuse Jem to reach me. I do remember the tightness of his grip and the tension in his muscles, and I remembered feeling even more ill for the worry I had caused him. I do not remember Cayuse Jem speaking with the Indians, though he must have. They must have explained to him that there had been no new cases of the fever in the last six days; that most of the stricken were well on the mend; and that, in a week to ten days, they would be well enough to travel, well enough to resume their normal lives. As for those whose fever had progressed further than the others...for those few...

I do not remember what was said, though I could not have known even if I could remember, for I do not speak their tongue. I do not remember Cayuse Jem lifting me in his arms and taking Boadicea's reins in his hand, though he must have done so, for I could not walk the way myself. I do not remember coming into the house, or what Cayuse Jem said to me, if he said anything at all. I remember waking in the tin bathtub. I remember being surrounded by warm, soapy water. I remember Cayuse Jem scrubbing me gently, washing me, tending to me. I remember that he spoke—I could hear the din of words—but I do not remember what he said, or even if I could comprehend him then. I remember moments of his touch. I remember holding my palm to his cheek. I remember hoping he understood all the sentiment such a gesture meant. I remember that it was all I was capable of at the time.

I do not remember being dressed in clean clothes, though I was. I do remember feeling unsoiled for the first time in quite some time. I remember Cayuse Jem saying something about food, and that I must eat. And then I remember nothing else, save blackness.

I woke to blackness as well, to the fixed dark of the middle of the night. I woke in our small bed, with Cayuse Jem pressed against me, keeping me warm, keeping me safe. I could feel the heaviness in his slumber and felt sure he had slept as little as I in these past seven days. But here I was now, home, home with him, and so he slept well. I was glad for it.

I had slept, yes, slept for a long span of time, but I had not slept well. I remember rising from the bed as quietly and cautiously as possible, so as not to disturb Cayuse Jem. I remember lighting a candle. I remember there was bread and cheese and milk, and I remember that my stomach was glad of it.

I do not remember taking out my journal, though as I am currently writing in it, it is evident I have done so. Perhaps the activity has become so rote to me that I do it without thought or memory.

Or perhaps I do not remember so many moments and events and happenings on this day because my mind is consumed by other thoughts, by other memories, by darker, more tragic, more horrible images than I had ever previously considered or known in my eighteen years of existence on this earth.

Motsqueh.

My brother, my companion. Chipmunk.

My friend. My only friend.

My only friend is dead.

19 September 1888

PHYSICALLY, I REMAIN unharmed by my ordeal in the woods.

I feel it important to mark that, since my current state cannot be a manifestation of some illness or injury.

Physically, I am well.

But I remain unwell in almost every other way that matters. In my heart, in my head...

I went to the woods to help my friend. To save him.

That is something I could not do.

I vacillate from bouts of great sadness to great rage. Rage at my own arrogance, rage at my own conceit. I am no doctor; that much was always clear. What rights had I to pretend otherwise?

Cayuse Jem has been most tender with me, most patient. He has let me rage when necessary and held me closely when I am wracked with tears. Over his gentle objections, I have tried to resume my life here on the ranch, but I find I can do no chores and contribute nothing meaningful, save taking care of Boadicea, my affectionate steed, who so adroitly cared for me.

Other than that, I sleep during the day and tend to be wakeful for most of the night. I cry. It is left to Cayuse Jem to care for the horses and tend to the chores and cook and clean, which he does without complaint or protest.

There are moments in the day when I feel as though I do not have the vigor to lift my arms over my head.

But physically, yes, physically, I remain unharmed.

21 September 1888

A MESSENGER CAME today from the Indian village, bringing news that was good and news that was troubling.

The good news was that Peopeo appeared to be well on his way to making a full recovery. When I left the village his rash had abated, and his tongue had returned to its normal color. The messenger reported today that the young lad's appetite had returned, and that his stools were more formed.

This was more than small comfort.

I gave thanks for the information and reminded the messenger that Peopeo must be kept on regimen, and that he should not have solid food for at least two more days. But the Indians already knew all this; I had repeated my instructions to Josefina *ad nauseam* before departing the camp. I told the messenger as well that another shipment of the quinine would come in a day or so, and that each member of the village must continue to take it, as a prophylactic against the fever.

He assured me they would do so.

The more troubling news concerned Chuslum.

He had taken Motsqueh's body deep into the woods. He refused the entreaties of the villagers to allow them to give Motsqueh a proper burial and refused to allow any of them to come near. The Indians were worried for his safety, for his life. They feared he would simply die of sadness.

I understood how that might feel.

Cayuse Jem listened closely to the messenger and spoke some words to him. Then he turned to me. "Boy, I need you to go home. Take care of the horses. I must tend to this. I will come for you later."

This made me fearful. "Sir, you cannot approach Chuslum, or Motsqueh, you may still yet catch the fever—"

"I know, boy," Cayuse Jem said, his hand squeezing my shoulder hard. "I promise to be safe. And I do not like leaving you. But I must help our friend." He lowered his voice and cupped my chin in his rough, calloused hand. "You've done such a good job taking care of everyone, boy. It's my turn now. Do you understand?" To be truthful, I did not, but I nodded nonetheless. "Go home. Take care of the horses. Eat. I will come for you near sundown."

I did not know what Cayuse Jem intended, but I did as he instructed. In a way, it felt good to be instructed, felt good to simply do as I had been told. I did my chores without pondering why I did them; I did them to care for the animals and to please Cayuse Jem, and in doing so, my mind found a blankness, an empty space behind the pain and the noise. Oh, I was not reciting the list of Popes or the Emperors of Rome as I worked, as I so often did, but my mind—at least for some duration of time—was cleansed of the blackness that had been its sole inhabitant for days. Yes, a void was decidedly preferable to the shadows.

All day long, I did not wonder what Cayuse Jem was doing, though his absence made me worry for him, and I hoped fervently for his safe and swift return. He finally came to me about an hour before sundown, as he had said. "Come, boy. It's time." And without another word, he guided me away from our home and into the woods.

I thought, for a few moments, we might be heading to the Indian village. It was a place I did not wish to visit;

indeed, I did not think I should ever like to go there again. But it was soon evident our destination was somewhere else in the forest—our swimming hole.

I choked back a sob as we journeyed on, and Cayuse Jem held my hand as we walked. As we approached the pool, I first saw Chuslum, kneeling at the base of a willow tree. And then I saw flowers, flowers of every sort and color and type as found in the territory, festooned around the base of a tree, the very same willow tree, in fact, that Motsqueh and I had lingered under on every occasion we had come to swim in the pool. And then I understood: Cayuse Jem had done this. He had come to this very special place, he had dug a hole in the earth, he had prepared the way for us all to say goodbye to our dearly loved friend.

He had even carved, into the base of the tree, Motsqueh's name and the year, and something else, a word in the Nez Perce tongue, a word I did not know but one I understood: beloved.

We stood there, the three of us, in great and grave silence. How long we stood I do not know. I know, after some time, I became cognizant of a presence. I turned and saw many members of the Indian village materialize from amongst the trees, all who had come to pay their respects to the youth who, in his life, I could only imagine had brought such life and joy to everyone as he did to mine. I saw Josefina, and we locked eyes for a moment and shared a small, sad nod.

It was the custom, I later learned, at Indian funerals, for the women and children to wail. But here, now, the group remained quiet, as silent as a forgotten tune, as silent as the day giving way to night. Chuslum, too, remained utterly still, and so did Cayuse Jem. But that was their way, the way of these men that Motsqueh and I loved with a boyish fierceness, with the totality of our beings and our souls. But silence was not his way, not my little friend, who ever more talked to me, even though I could not understand the words. And it was not my way, and not the way he saw me, his friend of letters, his companion of many words.

And so I spoke some words, words crafted by a better smith than I could ever be, words writ by another man who also once mourned the loss of a great friend:

> Yet once more, O ye laurels, and once more
> Ye myrtles brown, with ivy never sere,
> I come to pluck your berries harsh and crude,
> And with forc'd fingers rude
> Shatter your leaves before the mellowing year.
> Bitter constraint and sad occasion dear
> Compels me to disturb your season due;
> For Lycidas is dead, dead ere his prime,
> Young Lycidas, and hath not left his peer.
> Who would not sing for Lycidas? he knew
> Himself to sing, and build the lofty rhyme.
> He must not float upon his wat'ry bier
> Unwept, and welter to the parching wind,
> Without the meed of some melodious tear.
>
> For we were nurs'd upon the self-same hill,
> Fed the same flock, by fountain, shade, and rill;
> Together both, ere the high lawns appear'd
> Under the opening eyelids of the morn,
> We drove afield, and both together heard
> What time the gray-fly winds her sultry horn.
> But oh the heavy change now thou art gone,
> Now thou art gone, and never must return!
> The willows and the hazel copses green

Shall now no more be seen
Fanning their joyous leaves to thy soft lays.
As killing as the canker to the rose,
Or taint-worm to the weanling herds that graze,
Or frost to flowers that their gay wardrobe wear
When first the white thorn blows:
Such, Lycidas, thy loss to shepherd's ear.

I finished my dirge, and fat, slow tears fell down my face in testimony to my feelings for the lost youth. Cayuse Jem placed his arm across my shoulder and held me. Chuslum remained unmoving. I heard a slight rustle of leaves and watched as the last of the Indians receded into the forest, heading back to their village, giving Chuslum what he needed most—the time, and the space, to mourn his lost love.

Cayuse Jem and I did the same, walking to our house together, his arm never leaving my shoulder, my arm ever wrapped around his waist. We supped in silence and prepared ourselves for bed. I rested my head against Cayuse Jem's strong chest. I closed my eyes.

And, finally, I slept through the night.

24 September 1888

THE PAST FEW days have seen Cayuse Jem and myself fall back into our old routines, rising early, tending to the horses, mucking out the stalls. I have resumed the cooking—which has proved a balm to my soul as well as my stomach—and though I still have moments of sadness and grief, and am still prone to bouts of melancholy, I have found that our routine helps, and keeping busy helps, and, as always, having Cayuse Jem to care for, and to care for me, helps most of all.

I even laughed for the first time in a long time today, though it was not Cayuse Jem who made me do so. No, it was Boadicea who drove me to laughter. I was walking through the paddock when she approached me. I presumed she was looking for some attention, or a cube of sugar, and I gave her both. But she ignored the sugar and instead thrust her nose into my side and proceeded to nip at my shirt. This was a behavior I had never seen in her before. I stepped to one side, but she matched my movements, nipping at me and pushing against my side. "Boadicea," I said, "what is it, girl? What do you wish?" But no answer was forthcoming, and she proceeded to continue to push and nip and needle me to no end, bedeviling me as a gadfly might, chasing me around the paddock. Finally, with a more solid push, she tripped me and I fell, arse over tip, into the dust of the paddock. And then she proceeded to whinny and neigh in such a manner as if to laugh, as if to make semblance of a human laugh, and before I knew what I did, a smile broke my face, and the sounds coming from my lips matched hers, my own laughter matching hers. And then she brought her face down to my own and nuzzled my cheek with her nose, before moving her entire head behind my back and enfolding her neck around me.

As Cayuse Jem would say, that is her nature.

26 September 1888

EVERY MORNING FOR the last four I have prepared a basket of food, a basket of bread and cheese and meat, and every morning Cayuse Jem has hiked to the virid pool in the woods to leave it for Chuslum. He also takes with him a canteen of fresh water. And every evening Cayuse Jem makes a return journey to the pool, and every evening the basket comes back as full as it was sent.

The canteen is emptied, though I daresay Cayuse Jem only manages to triumph over Chuslum's despair in this matter through sheer will and force. But the man would not eat; that was clear. After four days it seemed evident he meant to do himself genuine harm, such was the depth of his loss.

So on this fifth morning I thought to try a different approach.

"May I bring Chuslum his food today, sir?"

Cayuse Jem gave his consent with a simple nod, a gentle squeeze of my hand, and a tender, lasting kiss on my forehead.

I brought with me more than just food and water. I brought soap and towels and fresh, clean clothing. I knew whatever spare raiment Cayuse Jem had would not be fit for Chuslum, but it mattered not.

I came to a halt as I approached the swimming hole. I swore I would never come here again. I swore that day we laid Motsqueh to rest, that day I sang the words of the blind poet over his bones, that I would never return to this place. What it had been, what it once meant to me, was lost forever. For a moment I hesitated, halting just a few steps shy of when I would first spy the tall, yawning arms of the willow tree. His willow tree. I took a deep breath and fortified myself.

And then I walked on ahead.

The flowers that covered Motsqueh's grave had wilted; a more apt memorial for mourning, perhaps, but not one that seemed to match the sunny, ever-merry disposition of my forever best friend. Chuslum lay beside the grave, prone and insert. He was pale and gaunt. It was evident he had not moved from this spot in days. Someone—I presumed Cayuse Jem, or perhaps one of the Indians from the village—had placed a blanket over him, to protect him from the cold of the night, but even now, in the pleasant warmth of the day, it still covered him.

I felt another presence here and heard a rustling of leaves despite the fact that there was no wind and no breeze. I turned to the tree line and saw one of the Indians from the village. So they, too, were keeping watch over their fallen companion. I knew the Indian had allowed me to catch a glimpse of him; if he had wished to remain unseen, he would have been able to do so at will. I recognized him as one of the scouts I had sent to search for the source of the fever. I nodded at him. He did not return my nod but held my gaze as he slowly receded into the forest and out of my sight.

I understood this message.

Once more, I was asked to play the part of healer.

I knew I could not fight with Chuslum, to force him to eat and drink and rise. Even in his shrunken state, I was no match for him. But I had no wish to fight. I approached slowly, reverently, but said nothing. I had no need of words.

I placed my basket and other goods to one side. Then, unhurriedly but deliberately, I lay next to Chuslum, positioning my form parallel to his own, slipping in between Chuslum and the grave of the boy he loved more than anything in the world. And then, reaching behind me, I took Chuslum's hand in my own, and draped his arm around my waist.

And then I did nothing else at all.

Instead, we rested there, he and I. I neither asked nor demanded anything of him. I merely stayed with him and shared in his grief and shared of my own.

I am unsure how long we lay there. The sun had passed its apex in the sky, though not by much, when I felt the first wracking spasm behind me. I held the Indian's hand tighter but moved not at all otherwise. Chuslum made no noise, but I could feel his body shudder and seize as he finally expressed some small fraction of his heartache and sorrow.

When his body ceased to clench and move, I shifted my own form into a seated position. Taking Chuslum by the arm, I moved him into an equivalent stance. Reaching into my basket, I broke off a small piece of cheese and gave it to him. Flatly, without perhaps any conscious effort, he ate of it. I gave him more cheese and some bread and a small piece of cooked meat. I did not give him too much; I did not wish him to take ill. If he has not regularly been consuming nourishment, then too much food at once could cause his belly to cramp, or worse. Mrs. Beeton recommended a posset of honey and wine for such occasions; I had no wine, but I could make due. And I will also prepare a cornmeal gruel, mixed with eggs and small, crispy pieces of pork fat, to begin to rebuild the man's strength.

I passed Chuslum the canteen, and I was contented to see him imbibe all of its contents. Then I stood and completely disrobed. I coaxed Chuslum to his feet and removed his buckskin trousers and his shoes. Grabbing him by the hand, I guided him into the pool. The water was much cooler than it had been the last time I was in it. I had a fleeting memory of Motsqueh, of laughing and playing with Motsqueh, but I pushed it from my mind. I led Chuslum several feet from the shore, until he was waist-deep in the water. Reaching over to the grassy bank, I took the towel from my bag, removed the bar of soap, and began to wash him.

First I wetted his entire body, his legs, his torso, his haunches, arms, and head. Then I took the soap, and foaming it generously in my hands, I rubbed it into his skin. I could see the grime of his torment falling off of him and into the still waters of the green pool in the woods. Moving behind him, I washed his back, his backside, and his legs. And then to the front, where I washed his stomach, his chest, and arms. I washed him once, and then twice, the first a gentle wash, the second a more vigorous scrubbing. Lastly, I bade Chuslum to kneel in the water, and I washed his long, dark hair.

Then I took him by the hand and guided him out of the water. I used the dry towel to rub him down once more, head to toe, and then dried myself as well. I dressed quickly, and slipped one of Cayuse Jem's large shirts over Chuslum's head. He was a tall man, so the shirt did not quite cover his entire midriff, but it would have to do. Cayuse Jem's pants were far too large for Chuslum, and mine far too small. I managed to craft a makeshift belt from a sturdy vine that grew at the far end of the pool and secured Chuslum in a pair of trousers. I placed Chuslum's shoes upon his feet and swept the hair out of his eyes.

I heard a rustle again and saw once more the Indian from the village. This time, when his eyes connected to my own, he returned my nod. I understood. Then he turned and walked back into the woods, heading home to his village.

And then, taking Chuslum by the hand, I led him home to the place that was now more home to me than anywhere in the world.

I brought him home to Cayuse Jem.

27 September 1888

CAYUSE JEM FOUND a space for Chuslum in the barn. He was of course welcome in the house—Cayuse Jem and I would gladly give up our bed to him—but he was not comfortable there.

"He still wants to be alone, boy," Cayuse Jem explained to me. "Just not as alone as before. Besides, he's not used to house living. He's lived in the open spaces his whole life." I set up a makeshift bed for him in the barn's loft. We had little spare furniture, so an old crate became an improvised stool, and Cayuse Jem hammered together some spare pieces of timber to make a small, crude table.

He sits with us at meals, breakfast and supper anyway. This evening, when we needed water from the creek, he took the pails from my hand and fetched the liquid himself. Cayuse Jem told me that there is much Chuslum can do on the ranch, if he likes, and that he has much experience with horses.

"I am sure we will be glad of any help he may wish to provide, sir," I said to Cayuse Jem, yawning as we prepared for bed. "I, for one, do not mind sharing my water-fetching duties."

Cayuse Jem gave me a small smile as he shucked his outer garments. He climbed into the bed, holding up the blanket and his inviting arms to me. I climbed in next to him. "How long do you think he will stay with us, sir?" I asked him.

Cayuse Jem shrugged. "I do not know, boy. He may be gone in a few days. He may never go." Cayuse Jem circled his arms around my waist. I could feel his warm breath and bushy beard on the skin of my neck. "Are you very sleepy tonight, boy?"

"Yes, sir," I said, drawing in a deep inhalation of air and closing my eyes.

Cayuse Jem kissed my cheek and then kissed me once more on the back of my head. "Then I shall wish you good night, boy. I love you."

"Good night, sir. I love you."

I lay in our bed for some time, my eyes closed, presenting myself to the world as sound asleep in the arms of my love. But it was merely a facsimile of slumber. I was not sleepy at all. I had lied to Cayuse Jem, for the first time ever, but I was not sleepy. But I understood what he wanted... I understood his wishes, and his intent, and I...I simply felt I could not acquiesce, could not give in to those...feelings...not now...

"We haven't really talked about it, boy." Cayuse Jem's voice surprised me. I had thought, by now, he would surely be asleep.

"Sir?" I said. There was no point any longer in pretending to be drowsy, so now my pretense suggested I did not know to what Cayuse Jem was referring. That, too, was a lie.

"We haven't talked about your—experience at the Indian village," Cayuse Jem started slowly, trying to tread sensitively on what he instinctually knew was delicate territory. "Of what you went through and saw and felt—"

"I do not wish to talk about it, sir," I said, interrupting. I hunched my shoulders forward and drew my arms into my chest.

"I know, boy," Cayuse Jem said softly. "But I think you must."

"Why, sir?" I asked. My voice had raised in pitch by nearly half an octave, and I drew in several great gulps of air. "Why must I?"

In response, Cayuse Jem took my shoulders in his hands and slowly, gently, spun me to face him. I half resisted this movement—though I could not articulate why I did—but I knew, too, that there was no resisting Cayuse Jem. The large man placed his thick, rough hand between my cheek and our pillow and held my face mere inches from his own. "Because it helps," he finally said. "That's why, boy. Because it helps to talk, even when you don't want to do it, even when you want to forget. Even when you think you don't deserve to feel better, it helps, boy."

Tears sprung from my eyes. I had become so accustomed to weeping these past few weeks, and I had grown to hate it. I wiped my eyes fiercely, as if the pressure of my hands might push the tears back into my body. "No," I said, but what I was dissenting to, I could not say. Cayuse Jem took my face in both of his hands and held me even closer. "No," I said again, and again, I could not articulate why I said it. It was not said to Cayuse Jem, and he understood that. He pressed his forehead to my own. I could feel his belly pushing into me. I could feel him, his totality and immensity, the warmth and heat and gravity of his love. I could feel him, and in that moment, for the first time in a long time, I could feel nothing else but Cayuse Jem.

I kissed him.

I kissed him without purpose, without consideration. I acted more out of a primal nature that demanded—nay, required—congress in that moment, that needed a union borne of love as balm and succor for my soul. So I kissed him, kissed this man I loved, kissed him with all the fervor and desire I had been suppressing inside of me these many days.

And he kissed me back.

Cayuse Jem's kiss contained less ardor and more restraint; he was seeking to understand the situation first, perhaps, before fully committing. He had wanted to talk, felt I needed to talk, and this was not talk. But it was communication; it was me opening up to the man I loved, and I think he soon comprehended the urgency of this particular need.

With much haste and fumbling, I removed his undergarments, and he removed mine. I shifted so that he would be on top of me, and lifted my legs to signal my most fervent desire. He held my ankles in his hands and used his own spit to lubricate his already engorged member. And then, he paused and peered at me, as if to ascertain that this act was, indeed, what I wanted and what I needed. I nodded, and without another word, Cayuse Jem pressed the tip of his member against my arse, and in one solid, well-practiced motion, he slid the entirety of himself inside me.

I am unsure what I expected to feel from this moment. Pain, perhaps? The adjudication of anger? A sense of punishment? An expulsion of what ailed me? But I felt what I had grown so used to feeling when I made love with Cayuse Jem—ardor, devotion, supplication, eros. And yet the sensation that most feverishly swept across me as Cayuse Jem penetrated my innards to his fullest capacity was relief, relief accompanied by release. Cayuse Jem was on top of me, pressing my knees against my chest, his member fully inside me. His lips pushed against my own, his beard tickling my clavicle, his large belly pressing against my stomach. The density of the man on top of me provided such tremendous comfort and respite. This was familiar, and good, and everything I longed for in the world at that precise moment in time. He thrust inside me, then out again, and then in once more. Cayuse Jem, the man, thrust into me, the boy, again and again, gaining steam, gaining momentum, harder and harder, thrusting harder and harder, and it was good. The weight of Cayuse Jem on top of me, the sensation as his turgid member nearly rent me in twain, the unioning of our souls—all of this, all of it, was the world to me. I had been denying myself this world—this act of congress, the good will and intent of this man who loved me so—as an act of punishment against my own self. As Cayuse Jem thrust into me, I felt a tremendous sense of liberation, a lifting in my spirit and in my soul that abated my desire for punishment and increased, instead, my desire to show, and to receive, love.

Our lovemaking on this night was not slow, and it was unaccompanied by the usual moans and grunts and declarations of devotion that always complemented this act for us. As Cayuse Jem spilled his seed in me, his thrusting belly rolled and reeled across my own engorged member so that I, too, spilled my seed, both at the same time. And then he lingered inside me, firm and warm and masculine and close, and he pressed himself on top of me so I might feel safe and protected and loved.

Afterward, Cayuse Jem cleansed me and held me and kissed me.

And I, I—at long last—began to talk.

"I should never have gone to the village, sir," I finally said.

"You saved many people there, boy."

"I did not save them all."

Cayuse Jem stroked my cheek with his hand. "I know, boy. I know."

Another damnable tear. "I was arrogant. And reckless. And foolish."

"Aye."

This surprised me. "You need not agree so readily!" I said, perhaps a bit more hotly than I intended.

Cayuse Jem stroked my hair with his hand. "But it was reckless to run into disaster like that. And what man but a fool goes toward a calamity, a plague? But you did, boy. And not because it is your nature to be reckless or foolish. Far from it. You did it to help."

"For all the good it did."

"For all the good it did—for all the good it did?" Cayuse Jem pushed himself up on his elbow. "You did a world of good, boy. I've knocked around this land quite a bit, and I've seen what this fever can do. Without your help, at least half of those people would have died. At least half. And many would have fled, spreading the disease to other tribes, to the other settlers in the area... Hard to say how many would have been affected. You prevented that, boy. You."

"But I am no doctor, sir," I said. "I'm just a dumb, arrogant boy with a book."

"You're a very smart boy with a book," Cayuse Jem corrected me. "Boy, do you understand what you have done? You did something I would never have done. Hell, I couldn't have done it, boy! You could. And what's more, you did." He paused, letting his last words sink in. "I sure don't know a lot of folks who would have done what you did. I don't know any, to be honest." Cayuse Jem dropped from his elbow and back onto the bed. "I'm proud of you, boy."

I pushed my shoulders into the broad, wooly expanses of his chest. "I was scared the whole time I was there, sir," I admitted.

"That only proves you're not a fool, boy. Only a fool wouldn't be scared of such a thing."

Cayuse Jem fell onto his back, and I twisted my body to fit perfectly into the crook of his arm. I leaned up to peer into his eyes. "Were you scared when I was gone, sir?"

Cayuse Jem ran his coarse hand through my fine hair. "Mighty scared, boy," he said. "Each and every day."

I lay my head against his cavernous chest. The thick, bristling hair on his torso comforted me. "Sir?" I had one last question. "If I did a good thing, then why do I feel so bad?"

"Because—" Cayuse Jem wrapped his thick, muscled arm around me protectively "—you're a boy, Nat, and you think with your heart. You're going to feel things all your life. It's just the way you are."

I pondered his words for a few minutes. "I think I'd like to go to sleep now, sir."

"Okay, boy." Cayuse Jem kissed the top of my head. "Good night, boy. I love you."

"I love you, sir." We lay there in the dark, the steady rise and fall of the man's barrel chest slowly, gently lulling me to sleep.

"Sir?"

"Yes, boy?"

"Thank you, sir."

Another kiss on my head. "Good night, boy."

28 September 1888

THIS MORNING CAYUSE Jem called to me from the barn. I came as bid and was surprised to see the Indians from the village—almost all of them—in force, standing next to our paddock.

I was caught completely unawares and stopped in utter surprise. The Indians stood utterly still, as if waiting upon me to do something, though I did not know what to do.

"Come, boy," Cayuse Jem said, motioning me to his side. I walked to him hesitantly, then stood beside him. My hands shook, a little, and I clenched them to quiet the motion.

The wizened old woman, the one I had appointed head nursemaid, stepped forward. Cayuse Jem pushed me two steps forward as well, so I was facing her. The old woman started to intone something in the Nez Perce language. As she chanted, she moved around me in a sort of shuffled dance. I heard the sound of a drum from somewhere amongst the throng of Indians.

I stood stock-still and swallowed hard.

When she finished, the old woman stood before me. She pulled a small leather pouch from her belt and reached two gnarled fingers deep inside. The pouch must have contained a red dye of some kind, for the old woman slowly rubbed two wide bands of the paint on my cheeks, one on each side. When she finished, I saw one of the village men stride forward. He was rather stout, with an amiable face, and still looked a little weak from his recent bout with illness. I recognized him as Josefina's husband.

He handed the old woman a garment of some kind. It resembled a jerkin. The old woman raised her arms, and I bowed as she slipped it over my head. The garment was elaborately beaded and seemed to bear some age.

Having completed her task, she turned to the rest of the Indians, raised her hands, and spoke a few words. The Indians gave a great roar in reply.

Then the old woman turned and spoke to me directly.

"I don't understand," I said to Cayuse Jem.

"They have made you a *tooat* and a member of the tribe," Cayuse Jem explained.

"A *tooat*?"

"It is a medicine man," Cayuse Jem explained. "And they have granted you a Nez Perce name: Peo Peo Hih Hih. It means White Bird." I must have still carried a confused expression, for Cayuse Jem added, "They are thanking you, boy."

"No—no," I said, moving to take the jerkin off of my form. "I—I don't deserve thanks, or any of this, really, I—"

"Boy." Cayuse Jem placed a strong, reassuring hand on my shoulder and squeezed. "They mean to honor you."

To honor me. And I knew I should honor them in return... I took a deep breath, gave a small bow to the old woman and mumbled my thanks to her.

The old woman crinkled her nose, smiled, and then shambled back amongst her people, who began to move off into the woods.

I was heartened to see Josefina did not join them right away.

"Are you well?" I asked her. "And everyone else? Are they quite well?"

"Oh, yes," she said with a broad smile. "The boy—Peopeo—has very much regained his appetite. And he will not be still for a moment. He is doing well." She peered over her shoulder at the old woman making her way to the woods. "She is his grandmother. That is why she honored you with the name Peo Peo. You are part of her family now."

I smiled sincerely; I took it as an honor, indeed. "And your husband—he is well? And you have enough quinine for everyone? And they are all taking it as directed?" Josefina gave me an indulgent look. "I am *tooat* now, Josefina," I added. "I have to ask."

"We have enough medicines. And my husband is very well. He is looking very much forward to when the baby comes." Josefina leaned forward and whispered in my ear. "If the baby is a boy, we shall name him Tiptip." A broad smile spread across my face, as broad as the horizon ignited by the setting sun. I was deeply touched.

"Chuslum is with you?" she asked me. It was Cayuse Jem who answered her, with a solemn nod, and Josefina nodded as well. "That is good. I know you will care well for him. You must tell him, though, we shall soon be leaving."

"What do you mean?" I asked.

Josefina wrapped a shawl around her shoulders. "It has become too hard to stay here. The tribe is worried about the water, the settlers... There is not enough of us, and not enough men. We shall go north, to the reservation. It is the only way."

I was sorry to see my friend go. "When will you leave?"

"We wish to leave before the snows come. The mountains will be difficult to cross. And the winter—" She shuddered at the thought of the winter to come and placed a protective, fretful hand on her belly. "But Peopeo and some of the others are not quite ready to travel such a far distance yet. They need more time to gather their strength. We go in two weeks, then, and will never return." She turned to Cayuse Jem. "You must tell Chuslum this. If he wishes to go with us, he must return soon." Cayuse Jem nodded. Josefina turned to me once more and took my hand in hers. "*Vaya con dios*, my friend."

"Goodbye, Josefina." I watched as she linked arms with her husband, and the two of them walked toward the tree line, back to the village, to prepare for the great journey ahead.

Cayuse Jem slid an arm around my waist and watched with me as the Indians melted back into the forest. "Will they be well, sir?" I asked.

"I don't know, boy. I hope so."

"Do you think Chuslum will go with them?"

"No." The certainty in his voice surprised me. He explained. "Chuslum would rather die than go to the reservation. He has always felt this way."

"Then he will stay with us, sir."

"He may prefer to be on his own, boy."

"That matters not." My certainty could not match Cayuse Jem's, but my determination surely could. "He is family. And he will stay with us." My voice softened. "Motsqueh would want us to take care of him."

"Aye, that he would." We turned on our heels and began to walk back to the barn. "You have a good heart, boy." I felt Cayuse Jem's hand slide down a few inches from my waist. "And a good arse, as well. You know, boy, I've never been intimate with a medicine man."

I smiled. It would appear that any resumption of my morning chores would have to wait.

30 September 1888

EACH TIME I write in my little journal I record the date at the top of the page. It is, by now, merely out of force of habit; I long ago stopped taking note of the actual date itself. At university, it was necessary to know each and every day of the week, to mark which class one is to attend, and when. My life was built around a schedule there.

But here there is more a routine than a schedule. Perhaps it is just the natural rhythm of rustic life. I could mark the end of a week by our bathing, but other than that, what care I for a particular date or day of the week? Such information had modest bearing for me, at best.

I was cognizant that summer had turned to autumn, but that mattered little for life on a horse ranch. We had no harvest to plan. Winter, I surmised, would have an impact on daily life here; but other than that, the machinations of spring and summer and autumn mattered little to life on the ranch.

But today I realized with startling clarity that it was the last day in September. That means tomorrow is the first day in October. And my father said he would come for me in October, in the mid-month period, to take me home.

But I am home. Being with Cayuse Jem is my home, the only home I shall ever wish for in my life.

When I commenced this journal I knew that the arc of my life was not my own to command. Then, I would have bargained the entirety of this life—my life—for a few years of study. Now...now, I wonder what I would not give for a few moments more being held by Cayuse Jem.

1 October 1888

LAST NIGHT WAS the most important night of my life.

After we made love, Cayuse Jem held me as usual, but there was a difference inside of me, in how I felt. Not in how I felt toward Cayuse Jem—nothing in the world could induce a change in that—but in what would become of us, of me.

Cayuse Jem could sense how ill at ease I felt. "What's wrong, boy?"

I have never truly pondered how simple and profound this question can be. Most of my life, when someone would ask me this very same question, I would dissemble and say nothing was wrong, not wishing to be burdensome, or not wishing to reveal any part of my true self. But I had learned by now to answer Cayuse Jem honestly and truthfully, whatever he asked.

"It is October first, sir," I said.

"And so it is, boy," Cayuse Jem prodded when I fell again into silence.

"I shall have to go home, soon, sir," I said.

Cayuse Jem tightened his grip on me. "You are home, boy."

I pushed myself as deeply as I could into Cayuse Jem's body; nowhere in the world could I imagine feeling more safe and loved. "My father will come for me, sir," I said. "Soon. For the wedding. I must—I must go back."

"Is that what you want, boy?" Cayuse Jem shifted, and I did, too, so that we may peer into each other's eyes. "Do you want to go back, to the fine house and those fine stables and all those other fine things I can never offer you?"

"No, sir!" I hotly replied. "I care naught for that, for any of that. I never have. I wish—"

"What is it you wish, boy?"

I swallowed hard. "I wish only to be with you, sir," I said. "I don't need anything but what we have between us."

Cayuse Jem smiled, and traced his thumb against the bones of my cheek. "Then that is what you shall have, boy," he said. "Boy, do you remember what I asked you that first night we came together?"

"You asked me if I understood what is happening between us, sir."

"That's right, boy. But I was not talking about our lovemaking. I was talking about our love." Cayuse Jem took my face in his large, brawny hands. "You belong to me now, boy. Body and soul."

"But my father—"

"I am your father now," Cayuse Jem said thickly. "I am your family. And I am your husband. If you will have of me."

I felt a fat roll of liquid escape my eye, a glistening portent of water that framed the wide smile of my lips. "Oh, sir," I whispered, too happy to voice any more reply than that.

Cayuse Jem took my hand in his and interlocked our fingers. "Then we are joined, boy," he said, his voice a low whisper like mine. "Now and forever. And what has been brought together in love, no man shall ever tear asunder."

And just like that, I have been wed.

10 October 1888

WHEN FATHER CAME to collect me for Dora's wedding, Cayuse Jem told him I was ill and highly contagious and should not be moved. Some fathers would have risked everything at that moment to see their child, to reassure their child that all will be well, to tell their child how much they are loved.

My father only turned his brougham around and fled as quickly as he could.

It is of no consequence. He ceased being my father some time ago.

Cayuse Jem sold half of his stock, purchased a wagon, and prepared for our trip. I thought we had everything we could possibly need, but I was wrong. Before we left, we made one last stop.

We went to my home.

To my old house, I should say, for my home now is wherever Cayuse Jem is. But there, at the manor house, when Father and Grandmomma and Dora and most of the servants were at the church for the wedding, we took the other things in the world that are most precious to me.

We packed up all my books.

I think even Cayuse Jem was surprised by how many books I had, but we put them all in crates and prepared for the journey. I also took everything else that was mine that could be sold: watches, jewelry, figurines. When your family mines silver, one tends to accumulate a veritable trove of small objects made of precious metal. We can sell these, and we will be off to a fine start in our married life.

Consider it my dowry to Cayuse Jem.

11 October 1888

THIS MAY VERY well be my final entry in this journal.

We are well on our way, Cayuse Jem and I. Chuslum is with us too. There was no discussion of his joining us, which was good: had he averred, I was prepared to show him how determined I can be in matters of honor, and in matters of family.

We made two stops ere we departed my father's land forever. The first was to Mr. Peterson. I had retrieved the deed to the property I owned from where I had secreted it in a book on—of all things—the geography and history of the Idaho territory. Rather fitting, I thought. And I knew the ideal individual to purchase the land from me.

We were a motley group knocking on the entry of the fine Peterson mansion. The haughty butler who opened the door could scarcely be bothered to ask our names. No matter. I am used to dealing with his kind.

"I am Nathanial Goldsmith," I said, "son of Jessum Goldsmith. And you will tell your master that I am here to betray my father."

Oh yes, that got us an audience with much haste indeed. Mr. Peterson veritably shook with glee at the thought of having the means to give my father a healthy dose of comeuppance. I sold the land to Mr. Peterson for a very reasonable price, though I extracted three conditions from him. The first was that I was paid all in cash. And the second was that Mr. Peterson would allow the Indians to remain on his land unmolested and untroubled until they left. And the third was that he would tell none of this to my father until they had gone.

After that, though...well, I think I should have enjoyed seeing the look on my father's face when Mr. Peterson informed him of his latest acquisition.

Our second stop was at the Indian village itself, where I told them of the sale of the land and presented them with most of the monies from said sale.

This was more money than the Indians had hoped to ever see in their lifetimes. And though they wished they had no use for it, they knew such monies would not only provide provisions to see them safely to the reservation, but that it could be used to see them through the winter and beyond, as well.

There was some small protest over the gift, but I quickly silenced them. I reminded the tribe they had made me *tooat* and it was my duty to look after my people. This was their land, by morality if not by right, and they had earned this lucre through toil and blood and tears.

And then I said my goodbyes and parted for a new life.

We shall go west and south. We shall sell our goods and precious objects along the way and purchase a small ranch somewhere. Cayuse Jem will raise Appaloosa, and I shall help him, as I always have. As for my books, well, Cayuse Jem laughingly suggests I should open a book shop. But I tell him I cannot part with anything so precious to me, and he smiles and laughs and wraps his arm around me and kisses me on my ear and tells me he understands.

There is, perhaps, one book I could part with. This one. I fear I was correct all along; I shall only feel the need to write in a journal when my life, itself, is not worthy of recording. This little tome helped to dull my initial worries and to lessen the tedium of my return to the territory. It helped me to overcome my fears, and my doubts, and to lessen some of the great pains I have endured along my journey's path. And it has been the official record of all the great joys and happiness I have experienced as well. But there is no more pain in me, and my life with Cayuse Jem could not be more full. I shall not imagine I will have much need of this little journal moving forward. I shall save it, of course, place it somewhere in my library, a reminder of the beginning of it all—the beginning of my journey toward self-awakening, the beginning of my story, the beginning of my life with Cayuse Jem. But it is a life, I believe, in which a journal like this will play no more part.

How happy that thought makes me.

18 September 1890

I ONCE JUDGED that I would never have occasion to write any more in this little journal of mine. Indeed, again, I am proven wrong.

Then again, a man can admit his mistakes. A man *should* admit his mistakes. I have learned this from Cayuse Jem.

I have learned so much from Cayuse Jem.

But this final entry is not being written for him. Or even for myself.

No, this is for you, Father.

I knew you would find me. You never accept loss and will not stand to be defeated. I knew you would send agents far and wide to track me down. And they could follow the trail of pawned objects, the trinkets you have presented me over the years as tokens of your esteem. One by one your agents could find these objects, and thus find the next step in our journey and, eventually, find me.

And so they have.

They will tell you what they found. But I am unsure you will believe them. Even though they will report what they see with their own eyes, and what I have told them with my own lips, you may choose to ignore what they say. And even if you do believe it, you still will not concede defeat. You will pursue me until you have wrenched me from my home and brought me back, a captive in chains, to submit to your resolve. Yes, I am to be Caratacus before the Emperor

Claudius, to make a great speech of redemption and bend myself to your will.

See, Father, I am still reading my books.

Indeed, your worst nightmare has perhaps come true: I am a proper bibliophile, or, rather, I am a librarian. After we left your lands, Father, Cayuse Jem and I and Chuslum settled in a small town along the borderlands of Nevada and California. And I sold everything you ever gave me, so that we might buy some land, a small ranch house, and some more stock. We even have a little money put aside, for what some might term a rainy day. Cayuse Jem raises the horses and still sells them to the same people he always has; apparently, Father, it is the trainer they valued, not the owner.

And so we have prospered.

As for me, well, I had so many books, and we had precious little space. So I took over the room above the town's postal office. But it is not a book shop, no; I could never part with any of my precious books. And the people in this town could hardly afford such costly commodities. Instead, I have made a library. And anyone in town who wishes to borrow one of my tomes is welcome to it. There is a generosity of spirit in lending my books that I am sure I never learned from you. And I am teaching the people to read as well. Anyone who wishes to do so may darken my door, and I happily accept them all as my pupils. There is no formal school here, so I teach almost all of the children, and many of the married women have come too. Even some of the farmers came, in winter time. They shall come again, next winter, and we shall pick up where we left off.

And I teach them more than reading. History, mathematics...even the natural sciences. And more useful subjects, like economics, animal husbandry, even agriculture.

I have sent away for books about farming techniques and household management, some quite technical tomes. And I read them, and in turn, I then instruct the people how to improve their crop yields or how to irrigate properly in drought conditions or whatever subject might benefit their lives.

It is amazing what one can learn between the covers of a book.

So I am a teacher after all, as I always wished. And I have some very fine pupils. One of my students, by the name of Theodosia, has perhaps the keenest mind I have ever encountered—keener than my own, to be sure. She had had some learning prior to my arrival in this town—her father had taught her to read and to do some figuring before he died—but she has absorbed so much knowledge since I first came... truly, I have never seen anything more impressive in my whole life. She can discuss Shakespeare as astutely as any scholar, and her facility with arithmetic is beyond anything I have taught her. I have made her my librarian's assistant, but it is her company, and her conversation, I most enjoy. I have written to the state university in Reno about her, in hopes of finding her a scholarship to study there when she is ready.

After all, a mind is a terrible thing to waste.

Theodosia has a brother named Thomas. He is older than Theodosia by a year, and my junior by about the same. Sadly, he does not possess his sister's intellectual curiosity, nor her academic abilities. Indeed, I have a devil of a time getting him to keep up with his reading at all; I fear he shall never truly learn.

But then again, we must all follow our own natures in this life.

Cayuse Jem has hired Thomas as a ranch hand, though the lad shows about the same talent for horses as he does for books. He is rather a tall lad—just as tall as Chuslum, in fact, though I would surmise he is only half his weight. I daresay I have not seen a skinnier boy in all my life, though he can eat as much as any horse. Any nourishment I place before him is devoured in record time; indeed, I have taken to guarding my own meal rather diligently, lest I turn my attention for too long and find some of it on the sharp end of Thomas's fork.

Theodosia and Thomas's father died when they were still quite young; their mother has been ill for some time. There is little my pharmacopoeia can do for her, since her illness appears to be in her head, and not in her body. The family was desperately poor, since they had no reliable source of income. The townspeople cannot afford to support the library or the school as a general rule, and, indeed, I neither ask for nor require anything from them but their curiosity and their diligence. But these are proud, good people, Father, and so they provide what they can, when they can. Eggs, extra butter or bread, on rare occasion spare coins—whatever they can give, they do. And I send it all home with Theodosia, every afternoon, so she and her mother are well nourished and need not worry about their next meal, or the next day.

As for Thomas, well, Thomas lives with us now—it is natural a hand should live on the ranch. We have taken to calling him Sweet Tom, for he is a sensitive, caring youth, even if he is rather harum-scarum, and clumsy to boot. He can never fetch a pail of water without tipping at least half the pail, and his feet are so large that he often trips over them if he is not paying close attention. But he is a good lad, a hard worker, and he tends to our vegetable patch as if the plants were his own children. And our vegetables have done very well, though I have oft said to Cayuse Jem that what seemingly most interests Sweet Tom in the vegetable patch is that he plans to devour every last morsel when harvest time comes.

Sweet Tom has grown quite close to Chuslum. They live together in the loft over the barn, and I sometimes hear them having long conversations deep into the night. Well, I hear Sweet Tom, mostly, as the lad does enjoy prattling on, and Chuslum was never one for conversation. But he did ask me to teach him English, and he is learning it well. Their bond is really quite touching. Sweet Tom always seeks out Chuslum to teach him any new task on the ranch, and the two go for long walks together in the evening. The lad looks up to the Indian and realizes there is much the older man can teach him. After we lost Motsqueh, I am sure Chuslum thought he would never have occasion to love again. But it appears Sweet Tom has worked his way into Chuslum's heart, and it is evident the strong Indian has taken great interest in the sensitive young lad. And it is just as evident that Sweet Tom admires and adores Chuslum with all his heart. I only wish the Indian would hurry up and bed the young man already. Cayuse Jem tells me these things take time, as it did with he and I, but our own lovemaking has been curtailed, constrained to our own bed in the evening, after dark, after everyone has retired for the night. I miss our sporadic but stirring midafternoon encounters in the barn— though, I must admit, we have once, or twice, or thrice, stolen into the loft ourselves—when Chuslum and Sweet Tom are busy with work—to enjoy each other carnally.

These are happy times, indeed.

So this is who I am, Father; this is my life now. I am in my library every morning, all morning, except, of course, for

Sundays. I loan my books to any and all who desire to read them. And then we discuss them, and we learn together. And the people are truly happy to have a town library and a school, and they embrace the eccentric young man who runs them both.

In the afternoons, I have my chores on the horse ranch. By the way, Father, I am quite the equestrian now. Cayuse Jem is proud of me and tells me often. He is by far the best teacher I have ever had, the best husband, the best family, and the best father, too.

In the evening, I cook meals for Cayuse Jem. (Actually, I have become quite renowned as a cook in these parts; my gooseberry pie won a ribbon at the local fair this past August.) I sweep his floors. I kiss his thick lips every opportunity I get. I lay with him. I please him. Oh, how I love to please him. And he takes care of me in turn.

And it—all of it—is better, greater, than any life I could have ever known as the son of Jessum Goldsmith.

Motsqueh was my brother, my twin soul, and I miss him every day. But having come to know Sweet Tom, I cannot help but note the parallels in our lives. I was born to a destiny that prophesied greatness, but I wanted no part of it. Sweet Tom was destined for poverty and despair. Both of us were saved through the love of men who wanted nothing more from us than to be ourselves, to find our true natures, and to love them in return. After all, Cayuse Jem has no grand ambitions for me, save one—to be happy.

I suppose I look upon Sweet Tom as a younger sibling—a rather pesky, occasionally maddening and irritating younger sibling—but he is dear to me all the same. As are all my family. Theodosia. Motsqueh. Chuslum. Cayuse Jem.

Always Cayuse Jem.

I am sending you this journal so that you may understand. Oh, I have no beliefs that you will understand about myself and Cayuse Jem, that you will understand what there is between us. That this life is the greatest expression of my own existence that could possibly ever transpire, far greater than the lofty dreams you had for me. I am not so foolish as to believe you will understand any of that.

You are not capable of understanding, or of loving, after all.

No, it is my fervent hope that, in reading this, you shall come to understand what you gain to lose by seeking me out again. You see, there is another copy of this journal. Actually, there are several. Oh, yes, I have had plenty of time in my quiet library to write all that I see fit. And should you persist in your endeavors to bring me back home, well, there are many influential people in the territory who would be utterly scandalized to learn what truly happened to the only son of Jessum Goldsmith, the Silver Baron of the Western Lands.

I believe this is what Mr. Collins meant when he wrote about a destructive agent so terrible and so foul that we both possess the means for the annihilation of the other. Yes, you can ruin my happiness and ruin my life, if you so choose. But I can ruin your life too.

See, Father, there is much to learn from books.

Please do not think I am wholly uncaring in this situation. I am not. I took your past from you when mother died as she gave birth to me; I stole your future when I ran away. But I finally learned that I had to look after my own future, that I had to make my own way in the world, as my father before me. But I shall not leave you wholly empty-handed. Here is my advice, for all you may deem it worth:

marry again. Have another son. Or take Dora's child and raise him as your own. You take what you will, without consideration for anyone else, so why not take a human being? Only, if you do, raise him with a bit more kindness. Raise him with a bit more understanding. The end result is likely to be far better for you, as well as for him.

I must admit it rather ironic that if only you had let me complete my studies, I would have likely submitted wholly to your will in every other capacity. It is not usually my nature to "kick up a fuss," as Cayuse Jem might say. But I suppose, thanks to him, I have changed. It was not too late for me.

Perhaps it is not too late for you.

Or maybe I have not changed. Maybe I have simply become the individual I was always meant to be. Some weeks ago, after Cayuse Jem and I had made love, and as he held me in his arms, I thought back to your purpose in sending me to him in the first place. "Sir," I said to him, "have I yet become a man, as my father wished it of me?"

"No, boy," Cayuse Jem replied.

I confess this was not the answer I had been expecting. I had left my home. I toiled on the ranch. I had faced a bear and a fever. I had uncovered my nature. I had embraced my true self. And I had made something of that self in this world, something good and true and worthy of respect. "And why not, sir?" I asked.

"Because you will never be a man. That's not your nature. You're a boy. You will always be a boy." And then he kissed me. "You will always be my boy." And then he kissed me once more. "That is what I trained you for, from the moment you crossed my door. That is what I taught you to be." And then he made love to me again and spilled his seed inside me and the world—my world—was utter bliss.

So I am still a bibliophile, Father. And I am ever more than that. I am a teacher, and yes, I am that sniveling scholar—in my own way—as you always feared.

And I am a cook and a horse owner and a husband.

But I am not a man.

And oh, I am so happy not to be one.

I know that this journal, and this last entry, will cause you great angst and rage. I understand those reactions, Father. They are natural for you. They are part of your nature. But if you will take one small bit of counsel? Fight your nature on this one. Accept this loss. Let people believe I am dead. Perhaps, in time, you will feel I truly am. In the end, it will be better for you that way.

Do not seek me out again, Father. For—and I feel quite certain in this—you shall not like what you find.

You shall not like the boy I have become.

About the Author

Drew Marvin Frayne is the pen name of a long-time author (Lambda Literary Award finalist) who is finally taking the opportunity to indulge his more sentimental and romantic side. When not writing the author lives with his husband of 20+ years and their dog of 10+ years in a brick home in the Northeast.

Email: drewmarvinfrayne@gmail.com

Website: www.drewmarvinfrayne.jimdo.com

Other books by this author

Second Level
Room at the Inn
Connection to Christmas

Also Available from NineStar Press

Connect with NineStar Press

Website: NineStarPress.com

Facebook: NineStarPress

Facebook Reader Group: NineStarNiche

Twitter: @ninestarpress

Tumblr: NineStarPress

www.ingramcontent.com/pod-product-compliance
Lightning Source LLC
Chambersburg PA
CBHW050508190726
48284CB00003B/735